THAT HORSE
WHISKEY!

Other Avon Camelot Books by
C. S. Adler

ALWAYS AND FOREVER FRIENDS

C.S. ADLER has written over thirty books for children and young adults. At one time Carole Adler taught English in middle school in Niskayuna, New York, and she and her husband raised their three sons there.

Many of Adler's books have also been published in Japan, Germany, England, Denmark, and Austria. She won the Golden Kite Award and the William Allen White Award for her first book, *The Magic of the Glits,* and has since won other literary prizes. Her books have often been on the Children's Choices list and have been chosen for many state lists.

THAT HORSE
WHISKEY!

C.S. ADLER

AN AVON CAMELOT BOOK

For Jeanne Place,
who trained the real Whiskey
and whose expertise
made this book possible.
With thanks for all her friendship
and all the fun we've shared!

AVON BOOKS
A division of
The Hearst Corporation
1350 Avenue of the Americas
New York, New York 10019

Copyright © 1994 by Carole S. Adler
Published by arrangement with Clarion Books, an imprint of Houghton Mifflin Company
Library of Congress Catalog Card Number: 93-30196
ISBN: 0-380-72601-7
RL: 4.9

First Avon Camelot Printing: March 1996

CAMELOT TRADEMARK REG. U.S. PAT. OFF. AND IN OTHER COUNTRIES, MARCA REGISTRADA, HECHO EN U.S.A.

Printed in the U.S.A.

OPM 10 9 8 7 6 5 4 3

To the bright western star,
my granddaughter,
Jenna Gavrielle Adler

*T*he first thing Lainey did on the morning of her thirteenth birthday was listen. No whinny. No pounding of hooves. She slipped out of bed and checked the front yard from her bedroom window. No horse was nibbling the stringy paloverde tree or browsing on the ornamental grasses Dad had planted to give the effect of a garden in front of their desert home.

Of course, she told herself, they'd tethered her horse out back. Except what could they have tethered it to? There wasn't a tree or even a fence post in the area that was going to be Cobb Lane Development when Dad got the houses built. Nothing was out there but scraped earth all the way to the edge of the cactus-studded desert that continued up into the bony brown mountains.

Well, maybe her horse was still wherever Dad had bought him. Or he could be at Dodge's ranch because that was probably where they'd board him until Dad could build her a corral and shed. She hoped he'd picked a beautiful animal, a bay maybe, with a black flowing tail and mane, young and frisky.

Except a beautiful horse would cost a lot. Mom's voice echoed warningly in Lainey's head. "Your father's not getting rich from starting his own business, Lainey."

A colt, then, she thought as she got into her jeans. A horse too young to ride would be cheaper, and he'd still be Lainey's to train and care for and love. Oh, even if he were old and knobby kneed she'd love him because he was hers.

Ever since she had learned to ride when she was nine, Lainey had dreamed of owning her own horse like her friend Amber. On her tenth birthday Dad had given Lainey her lucky felt cowboy hat with the feathered band around the crown. "Someday there'll be a horse to go with it," he'd said. Last birthday he had given her a new pair of riding boots. "I'll get you that horse next year," he had said, fixing a time on the promise.

Today was next year.

She was pulling on the boots that she'd polished last night in honor of her birthday gift when the phone beside her bed rang.

"Did you get it yet?" Amber asked.

"Not yet. I just woke up."

"Yeah, well, hurry up. I'm dressed and ready to go riding in the wash with you this morning."

"Maybe it'll be just a colt."

"A colt? You've got to be kidding, Lainey. Your dad promised you a horse. I've got all these plans for where we'll ride this summer."

Lainey chuckled. Amber sounded as aggrieved as if she were the one being cheated. "Take it easy," Lainey told her. "Dad's never not come through for me. If he couldn't get me a horse, he'd have said and not let me keep hoping for nothing."

"Right," Amber agreed. "Okay, then, I'll be over in an hour to see what you got."

Clack went the phone in her ear. Lainey grimaced. Amber hadn't even wished her happy birthday. Never mind, Lainey told herself. Amber was honest and loyal and as passionate about horses as she was. They'd be friends even if Amber weren't the only girl within walking distance here on the outskirts of Tucson.

Lainey brushed her shiny, waist-length black hair into a single thick braid. Dad loved her hair loose, but the braid was better for riding. She picked up her lucky riding hat and hurried down the hall to the kitchen, where she could hear Mom's cool mountain stream of a voice crossing Dad's rumbling one.

"Morning, everybody. Here I am, teenaged at last. Do I look any different?" She twirled for them, posing with her hat out in one hand.

"You're a picture," Dad said, but his usual exuberance was missing.

When Lainey asked him, "Don't I get a birthday kiss?" he held out his arms silently. He was a big man, muscular from all the hammering and sawing he'd done. His hair was dark like Lainey's, but wavy, and his features were large where hers were small. Lainey kissed him and lingered in his hug. Dad was the big hugger and kisser in the family. He'd even hugged and kissed Lainey's older brothers before they'd left home for good.

Lainey waited, tingling with excitement, for something to be said about her horse.

"So what does the birthday girl want for breakfast?" Mom asked. "Pancakes?"

"I'm not very hungry," Lainey said. She never was, and she knew it bothered her mother, who enjoyed satisfying the huge appetites of the men in the family.

Apologetically, she went to peck her mother's smooth round cheek. Mom was blond, with a china doll face, big blue eyes, and creamy skin. She wasn't delicate, though. Her large, solid body seemed to compress the air, making it hard for Lainey to breathe near her. Small and slim as Lainey was, she felt in danger of being crushed close to her mother.

On her place mat—Lainey always sat facing the sliding doors to the patio—was an envelope with her name on it. She picked it up. It would be like Dad to hide the clue to her horse's whereabouts in her birthday card, just to keep up the suspense to the last second. "Can I open it?" she asked him.

"Why not? It's your birthday present," Dad said.

Instantly Lainey understood. He hadn't wanted to pick the horse himself. There'd be money in the card to buy it. The outside of the card showed a girl on a horse, and inside—inside was a hundred dollars. Not enough to buy a good horse, not even a good colt. Was this to pay for horse feed, then? Puzzled, Lainey looked at her father and asked, "What's this for, Daddy?"

"Riding," he said. The rumble in his voice was heavy, and his eyes squinted at her as if he were in pain. "Buy you some riding time at Dodge's. There's no horse, Lainey."

"No horse?" She stared at him in disbelief. "But Daddy, you said—"

"I tried. Couldn't swing it. Not yet. I'm sorry, honey. I'm really, really sorry." He looked down at his plate as if he couldn't face her.

She turned to her mother. "Is he joking?"

Mom's eyes were sad as twilight. "Times are hard right now, Lainey. You know houses aren't selling. I told you there's no money."

"You didn't tell me. You just said—and Daddy, you didn't say anything. You told me I was getting a horse. If you changed your mind, why did you let me keep hoping?"

"I was sure things would look up and we'd swing it for you somehow."

"Lainey," Mom said sharply, "you know your father would give you the moon if he could." She was on Dad's side, as always, in any situation.

"I didn't ask for the moon, just a horse. And you promised." Lainey stared hard at her father. Betrayal had emptied her of everything but anger. "You shouldn't have let me keep hoping, Daddy. That was mean."

The room looked smaller when Dad stood up. Shadows etched his face now. "I'll see you ladies tonight," he said. "Got a good hour's drive to that addition I'm supposed to be building." He glanced at Lainey and his lips formed words, but he strode out to the carport without speaking them.

The air conditioner clicked on even though it was still early morning.

"Mom!" Lainey cried and burst into tears.

"I'm sorry, Lainey," Mom said. "But you made your father feel worse than he already does. A horse is a luxury, and right now we're having a hard time paying for the essentials. There just isn't any business. Every deal has fallen through. Even remodeling work is hard to get."

"But why didn't he tell me that?"

"Because he doesn't like to worry you. He wants you to enjoy your childhood."

"He treats me like a baby. He always has. I hate it. I hate—" Lainey choked on her rage.

"Get a hold of yourself now," Mom said. "And tonight you better apologize to your father, and sound as if you mean it. Or else."

Lainey bolted from the room and ran to her own. She threw herself on her bed. Apologize to him when he'd deliberately let her go on expecting, when he hadn't trusted her with the truth?

The sliding door in the kitchen whispered open, and Amber's voice said, "It's me, Mrs. Cobb." Lainey sat up and dried her wet cheeks with her sheet.

If she'd been one of her older brothers, Dad would have leveled with her months ago. Then she would have had time to ease into her disappointment. If he'd just said, "Soon as I sell a few of the houses in this development, Lainey," or "Soon as I get more remodeling jobs. . . ." Her brothers claimed she was Dad's favorite, but they were the ones he'd asked to join him in Cobb Builders. They were the ones from whom he expected the most—until Lon had left to join the air force and Pete had run off to New York City to be a musician. She might be Dad's favorite, but he didn't respect her. That was what she couldn't forgive him for.

"Lainey, your mother told me," Amber said. She was standing in the doorway in her riding outfit, her square freckled face shaded by her Stetson and her blond hair cropped so short she looked like a boy. "Look," she said, "why don't you rent a horse from Dodge's and we'll go riding anyway. No sense wasting your birthday altogether."

"No," Lainey said. She didn't have the energy to ride this morning.

"Come on. I'll treat you," Amber insisted. "I was going to get you a present anyway—something for your horse. So instead, I'll treat you to rent."

"No." Lainey shook her head. She knew Amber's father was rich from his car dealership, but when Amber offered to pay for things, it made Lainey feel less than equal. "You go alone, Amber."

"So you're just going to lie around and sulk?"

Stung, Lainey answered, "I'm going to figure out how

to get enough money for a horse. I'll just have to save up and buy my own."

"Save up what? Your allowance? You'll be an old lady before you have enough. You know Belle cost my dad over a thousand dollars. Even if you buy a colt, you're talking hundreds."

"I've got a hundred to start, and I can earn money."

"Oh, sure. What can you do? You tried babysitting already." Amber snickered.

Lainey bit her lip, recalling that humiliating day when she'd been locked in the closet by the Wilsons' twin boys and didn't get out until their parents came home and released her. Amber had laughed so hard when Lainey told her the story that Lainey had seen the humor in it and laughed with her, but it didn't seem funny now. What *could* she do? There were only a few houses along the highway near enough to walk to. Amber's twelve-room ranch house, with its kidney-shaped swimming pool and the barn and corral where Amber kept her horse, was a half mile away. Dodge's ranch was a quarter of a mile in the other direction.

"Well, maybe Mr. Dodge will hire me," Lainey said.

"You're going to become a wrangler?"

"The cowboy he hired a month ago quit on him this week."

"But, Lainey, you're just a kid."

"He lets me saddle my own horse sometimes," Lainey argued. "He says he knows he can rely on me to do it right. He likes me, Amber. He says I'm good with the horses."

"Okay, so ask him, and while you're there, rent a horse and come with me. I'll *lend* you the money if that's the only way you'll take it."

Lainey considered. It *was* her thirteenth birthday, after all. But she'd have to pay back any money she borrowed, and that was no way to save. Besides, Amber never cared how many hours she rode. She'd keep going even into the hundred-plus temperatures of Tucson's summer afternoons when every living creature was resting in the shade. "I think you'd better go without me," Lainey finally said.

"You're no fun," Amber said. "Okay, be a pain. See if I care." She stomped off down the hall in her cowboy boots. A horse snorted outside. No doubt Amber had left Belle standing with her reins dropped to the ground. She was proud of having trained Belle to be ground hitched.

So now Amber was angry at her. Up for barely an hour and already Lainey had set everyone against her. Some way to celebrate her birthday.

Mom filled the doorway suddenly. "I'm going to the trailer to get those specs ready for your father. Want anything before I leave, Lainey?"

"No, thanks."

"Well, you be done sulking by the time your father gets home tonight. He's depressed enough as is."

"I didn't know that," Lainey said.

"Now you do." Heavy as Mom was, her footsteps were light as she walked away down the hall.

With a sigh, Lainey got up. She'd better do her thinking on her way to Dodge's ranch because if she meant to impress him, she'd have to arrive early.

Outside in the hazy yellow morning air, Lainey looked around. There wasn't much to see on the bare desert landscape. Theirs was the only house finished in Cobb Lane, but the gravel roads were in. Their curves and little flags indicated the lots on which houses would be built someday. Two partially built models were waiting for buyers.

Next to the adobe arch with the words *Cobb Lane* incised on it was the trailer office where Mom would sit waiting for the telephone to ring. Mom was the salesperson and sole office staff for Cobb Builders. Awful boring work, Lainey thought. Planning and design would be more interesting. Even carpentry had to be better than office work.

She hadn't yet told Dad that her ambition when she grew up was to be the child who made the *s* at the end of Cobb Builders mean something. What if there were no business for her to work in when she grew up? Poor Dad. He'd talked about being his own boss for so many years, and he'd cracked the champagne bottle against that adobe arch with such high hopes. Lainey had been sure they were going to be rich any minute. Well, he should have told her things were bad. She wasn't a baby, and he shouldn't still be treating her like one. Never mind. Buying her own horse would convince him of that.

Hat set squarely on her head, Lainey set off for Dodge's ranch.

2

*J*ust past the plantings of yucca and tall saguaros and fake rocks that were supposed to help customers see the potential charm of Cobb Lane Development, Lainey saw Mr. Dodge's head wrangler coming toward her. Lopez was riding Chico with his usual straight-backed grace and leading a trail ride of what looked like businessmen. They were probably from some convention at the big new hotel a mile past Dodge's ranch. The hotel had been set in foothills studded with cholla and mesquite trees and creosote bushes so unpalatable nothing else would grow near them.

Lopez would be taking the men to the wash, where they could gallop in the dry sandy riverbed for an hour. Or maybe he'd lead them across the road for a walk on one of the state forest trails, out there where sharp-edged mountains took up all the space that wasn't sky.

"Hi, Lopez." Lainey greeted the small, elegant man with respect. He knew more about horses than anyone—more than Mr. Dodge himself by his own admission.

A nod was all Lopez granted her in return, but Lainey didn't feel slighted. Lopez did his communicating with horses, and even then in silence. She wondered if it was for his horses that he kept his pearl-buttoned western shirts immaculate and his pointed cowboy boots freshly shined.

To Lainey's surprise, the last rider in line was mounted on Whiskey. Now why had they sent out Whiskey this early in the day when they still had all of Dodge's horses in the corral to choose from? As usual, Whiskey came abreast of Cobb Lane and promptly reversed course to gallop home. A quarter of a mile was the powerful brown horse's limit. Even Lopez couldn't make Whiskey go farther.

The hefty, thick-legged man riding him seemed to know what to expect because he immediately began tightening the reins and trying to turn Whiskey back in the direction the other horses were going. Once he'd forced Whiskey's head around, the man dug in his spurs. Lainey winced. She hated spurs—the cruel bite of their steel cutting edges. The spurs and the high curved bit on Whiskey's bridle were meant to hurt him. Not to mention that the jowly man must weigh a ton.

Again he dug his spurs into Whiskey's belly. Instead of giving in, Whiskey reared, but the man kept his seat.

"Ride 'em, Marshall. Whoopee!" yelled a pale young man with a newly hatched look.

"Get down, you sucker. I'll show you who's boss," Marshall snarled.

Whiskey twisted and reared again without unseating his rider. A vicious jab of the man's spurs made the horse scream. Lainey's heart squeezed in a fist that released only when Whiskey finally managed the turn and kicked up his heels for home. In an instant, horse and rider were toy sized in the distance.

"We'll wait here," Lopez told the other four men quietly. "There's another horse saddled and ready for him."

"Well, Marshall can't say he wasn't warned," a pudgy rider said. "That horse did just like you said he would."

"Aw, Marshall will master the sucker yet. Bet ya," the young man said.

"Master that outlaw? Not a chance," the pudgy man said.

By then Lainey had walked out of hearing range. A while later, she turned into the gravel driveway in front of Mr. Dodge's ranch house. The building was so old it had no air-conditioning. It was protected from the sun by its own thick walls, plus the shade of an enormous tree, and the ramada—a long front porch with a roof of woven sticks.

Whiskey was rearing and bucking in front of the ramada. The man they'd called Marshall gave a mighty yank on the tight reins, forcing Whiskey's head up. The horse's mouth was open and foaming. He bellowed as Marshall cut into him with his spurs.

Lainey wanted to scream in sympathy.

Mr. Dodge stood on the ramada, pleading in his old-man's quaver for Marshall to take the horse already saddled and tied to the rail outside the barn and leave Whiskey be, but Marshall wouldn't stop. Suddenly Whiskey bolted and slammed sideways into the wall of the barn. The big man howled and fell off the horse.

Lainey brought her clenched fists down on her thighs. "Good," she said to herself. "You got what you deserved, Mister."

Whiskey was soaked in sweat and wild-eyed. He trotted to the corral fence and effortlessly jumped it. Safe inside, he trotted past the other horses feeding on the hay the cowboys had pulled from the bales stacked inside the feeding station's protective fence. He stopped in front of the water barrel, shook himself, and began drinking.

Mr. Dodge was bending over Marshall. "I knew this was going to happen," the old man wailed. "I knew it. You hurt?" He offered Marshall an arthritic hand to help him up.

"I think my leg's broke," Marshall moaned.

Lainey slipped through the corral gate and walked toward Whiskey. He wasn't a horse she'd ever ridden, but she had seen Lopez moving him around and saddling him without apparent difficulty. Some horses tried to nip you if you weren't wary, but Whiskey didn't bite or kick. He just didn't choose to be ridden more than a quarter of a mile.

"There," she said, "you showed that big lunk who

was really boss, didn't you, Whiskey?" She stroked the animal's damp, pulsing neck. He kept his nose in the water barrel, ignoring her, but his dark chocolate hide flicked with nervous tension. She kept talking and stroking anyway to calm him.

"You're not a bad actor, are you? You just don't like bullies, right, Whiskey? I don't blame you one bit. No, I don't. He was gross, that man."

Whiskey twitched his ears. He lifted his nose from the water barrel, and a warm brown intelligent eye fixed on her under its curve of black lashes. She kept stroking and talking, and when he didn't move away from her, she risked walking behind him to get to his other side where she could undo the cinch. Deftly, she slid his saddle and blanket off.

"Come on," she said, setting the saddle, horn end down, on the ground. "Let's get that bit out of your mouth and you'll feel better."

He let her remove the bridle. Then he blew out some air and walked away from her to the far side of the corral.

Mr. Dodge's Jeep was just pulling away from the ramada with Chick at the wheel and Marshall in the backseat. Chick saw Lainey and waved. The baby-faced wrangler with the long blond hair was Lopez's opposite, young enough to be his son, for one thing, and puppy dog friendly where Lopez was dignified and cool. But the two worked well together.

"Lainey!" Mr. Dodge called from the ramada. "What are you doing in there? That beast steps on you and I'll have your dad suing me along with that Kansas City cowboy who just busted his leg."

"He's not really going to sue, is he?"

"Can't say. We told him the horse was no good, told him even Lopez couldn't make him go, but the fool wouldn't listen," Mr. Dodge said. "Chick's taking him to the emergency room to get the leg set. Leaves me shorthanded, and I got another group going out this morning. Guess I'll have to lead them myself."

Mr. Dodge lifted his cowboy hat with one finger, exposing a band of white freckled forehead above the tanned part of his wrinkled face. "Soon as I get a minute I'm going to put an ad in the paper and sell that fool animal for whatever I can get for him. Worst comes to worst, I'll sell him for dog food."

"Whiskey's too young and beautiful to be made into dog meat," Lainey protested.

"He's a useless, no-good, ornery beast."

"He could be trained."

"Not likely. If Lopez can't do anything with him, nobody can." Mr. Dodge shook his head. "I got took when I bought that horse. Should have ridden him first instead of just looking him over. Serves me right for getting careless. . . . Did you want to ride this morning?"

"What I really want is a job," Lainey said quickly. "You're shorthanded and here I am, ready to start."

Mr. Dodge's milky blue eyes smiled at her kindly. "I wish I could hire you, Lainey. You'd be worth more for sure than that no-'count fellow who just quit on me.

But you're too young. Besides, you're too small and female to do the heavy work around here."

"I can do anything that kid did for you," she insisted, stung by the small-female label. Being young would change, she knew, but being small and female never would.

"Lift heavy bales of hay and fifty-pound feed bags?" Mr. Dodge's weathered face was split by a laugh. "Come on, honey. I know you're game, but you don't weigh more than eighty pounds yourself."

"I can move heavy things with a wheelbarrow. And I can saddle up any horse here, and I can groom and feed them and muck out the stalls when they need to stay inside. I could lead trail rides, too, if you'd let me."

"No, no, Lainey. Maybe when you're grown, but now. . . . How did your birthday go? You get your horse?"

Lainey ducked her head. "No, Dad can't afford one right now."

"Times are tough. Yeah," Mr. Dodge agreed. "Well, tell you what. I got a kid coming today. Raised by his mama in New York City. Real city boy, despite his dad grew up here in Tucson. Don't know how I let myself in for this one." Mr. Dodge shook his head in wonder at himself. "Except his dad helped me out once when I needed a hospital bed in a hurry. He's director of the hospital. Anyway, I promised I'd teach this kid to be a cowboy in exchange for whatever work I can get out of him."

Lainey waited patiently for the old man to get to the point. "Boy's late already. They sure don't get up with the chickens in New York City. No sir." Mr. Dodge laughed as if he'd made a joke.

Lainey smiled politely. What did this boy have to do with her?

"Or maybe the kid missed his plane," Mr. Dodge said. "Supposed to get in last night. That could be why he's not here yet."

Lainey hoisted Whiskey's saddle and balanced it on her hip. "What were you going to tell me, Mr. Dodge?" she asked to remind him. "You said, 'Tell you what.'"

"Oh, so I did. . . . Well, Ryan. That's his name. Ryan. Seeing as I'm short on wranglers to show him the ropes, how about you take him in hand, and I'll pay you off in free riding? How'd that be?"

Free riding wasn't the cash payment Lainey had hoped for, but it was a step toward convincing Mr. Dodge he needed her. "Great," she said. Then more cautiously she asked, "How old is Ryan?"

"Somewheres near your age." Mr. Dodge's head jerked as a Range Rover pulled up to the ramada and a man with thick, curly, graying hair leaned out the window on the driver's side.

"Here he is, Dodge," the man yelled. "Son of a gun overslept on me. Of course, it's 5:00 A.M. back East, so you might give him a second chance to prove he's not lazy."

A tall, husky boy got out of the passenger side of the

18

car. He stood there, dark haired and serious as a carved totem, with his eyes fixed on the driver.

"Pick you up after work, son," the man said to him. "I know it's not hospitable to dump you, but I'm late for a budget meeting that won't go without me."

The boy held his stare without saying a word.

"Yeah, you'll be fine," his father concluded. He gunned his engine, backed up, and roared off onto the highway toward town.

"Ryan!" Mr. Dodge called. He held out his hand, and the boy shambled over reluctantly to shake it. "Welcome to Tucson. So you want to be a cowboy, do you?"

"No way," Ryan said. "I only came out here to get to know my father."

"That so?" Mr. Dodge said. "Well, then, he must be the one wants you to be a cowboy."

"I'm satisfied being what I am."

Despite the resentment in Ryan's eyes, Mr. Dodge kept his smile going. "You're lucky," he said. "Me, I'm not satisfied being so old, and Lainey here, Elaine Cobb—she's going to show you what's what today— she's not satisfied being a girl."

Lainey's jaw dropped. Could Mr. Dodge read her mind? She'd never admitted to anyone that she sometimes thought she'd have been better off if she'd been born a boy.

Ryan's wide hazel eyes focused on her. She hoped his anger was at his father and not at being assigned to her. He had to be at least fifteen or sixteen, and unless his bulky body was all flab, he wasn't going to have any trouble heaving bales of hay and bags of feed around. Maybe he'd even get paid for working after she'd trained him. Probably would, she thought bitterly, even if he·didn't appear to appreciate his good fortune.

"Well then, Lainey, for starters, why don't you take Ryan along to the tack room and show him what goes with what?" Mr. Dodge said. He was obviously eager to be rid of his charge so he could get to work.

Before Ryan could protest, Lainey turned and entered the barn, still hauling Whiskey's saddle and bridle. She was glad to hear footsteps behind her. After all, if she could earn riding time, she could put her birthday money toward buying a horse. And who knew what other odd jobs she might pick up?

She hoped Ryan turned out to be a slow learner. If Lopez and Chick were too busy to teach him much, she might earn a *lot* of riding time.

3

*T*he tack was kept in a small dark room beside the stalls where the lame or ill horses spent their sick time in the barn. It was a musty, coolish place. The wranglers liked to hang out there during the hottest hours of the afternoon while the horses rested outside in the shade of the shed roof. In the tack room, the men would busy themselves repairing and cleaning the leather bridles and saddles. Lainey sniffed the ripe, gamey perfume of oats, oiled leather, and horse dung, and then got down to business.

"If you're wondering about these coffee cans sticking out from the wall, Ryan," she began, "they're for hanging bridles over. And see these snaffle bits here? They're used on easy horses like Lady and Shiloh, but horses with harder mouths get—" She looked back to see if she had Ryan's attention.

He was staring out the lone window, leaning against the frame with his arms folded across his chest. But the window was too dirty to see through, so what was he staring at?

"Ryan?" she said. "Are you still asleep?"

He shifted his eyes her way. "So what if my father's a big shot? He could've taken a day off to spend with me—my first day here. It's not like—I didn't even recognize him at the airport, and he wouldn't have recognized me if Mom hadn't sent him one of my school pictures."

"You don't even know your father?" She was shocked.

Ryan shrugged. "Mom left him when I was born. I've never met the guy. Except he came to New York once when I was two or three. I don't remember that, though."

Lainey didn't know what to say. All of a sudden she understood Ryan's anger and she felt for him, but she couldn't imagine having a father and not knowing him.

Ryan swallowed audibly. "I just want to talk to him," he said. "Just talk. I'm not here to be turned into some stupid imitation cowboy."

She was afraid he was going to cry. "Did you tell him how you feel?" she asked.

"No," Ryan said. "He hasn't let me tell him anything. When he picked me up at the airport last night, he went on about why my plane was so late—like it was my fault he had to wait so long. Then on the way to his house, he filled me in about his job and how he's got to be at the hospital all hours just like the doctors."

A horse whinnied outside in the corral. Ryan glanced toward the window before going back to what he was saying. "Then he dumps me in a bedroom without a reading light." He gave a half grin and added, "I guess that sounds stupid, huh? I mean to care about a reading light."

"No," she said, wanting him to continue. "No."

"This morning he rolled me out of bed and handed me a mug of coffee and a doughnut to eat while we drove over here. On the way he gave me a lecture about how western kids grow up knowing how to handle a horse. Like growing up in New York City makes me an automatic wimp."

Lainey took a breath and launched into the kind of sensible, logical response her mother always offered to anything emotional. "Probably your father just doesn't know how to talk to you. Probably he's nervous about how the two of you'll get along."

"Yeah, well, I'm not going to get along with him if he's not going to spend any time with me. He shouldn't have invited me out here if he didn't have the time. I did just fine without a father for thirteen years, and I don't need one now."

"Thirteen? You're just my age? You look so much older." She meant to flatter him, but his answer was mocking.

"I probably am older—light-years older mentally."

She drew herself up stiffly. "What gives you *that* idea?"

"Because you're a horse groupie. Girls that love horses are usually not big on world affairs or literature or—what do you read?"

"I read," she said.

"Yeah, but what?"

It was a test, and though she resented it, she guessed if she failed to answer, he wouldn't accept her as his teacher. Taking a deep breath, she tried to remember the last book she'd read. "Umm, biographies. I'm reading a biography of Sally Ride right now. You know who she is?"

"Sure," he said. "I'm familiar with American folk heroes, even female ones." He smiled, a smile so appealing that she held off hating him even when he asked, "What else?" as if he expected to trap her on this one.

"I'm not a big reader," she admitted straight out. "I'm going to be an engineer when I grow up. I like math and science; I'm an okay student, but—and how about you?"

"Well," he said, "on summer vacation I look forward to going to the library, bringing home a stack of books, and holing up in our nice air-conditioned living room to wallow in literature. You think that's weird, don't you?"

She couldn't answer without insulting him, so she sidestepped the question. "Maybe your father's afraid you'll get bored while he's at work. I mean, that could be why he wants you to learn about horses."

"If he'd asked, I could have told him I already know all I need to know about them."

"You do?" That was a direct hit to her hopes.

"Sure, Mom sent me to summer camp and I rode there."

"English or western?"

"You mean the saddle? It had a horn."

"Western," she said. "Well, do you know how to saddle a horse?"

"No. My mother paid a bundle so I wouldn't have to do any dirty work."

"Out here people get respect for what they can do with their hands," she advised him sternly.

"Tell me," he said, "what are you supposed to get out of showing me how to saddle a horse?"

"Depends."

"On what?"

"On how much you need to learn." She didn't know whether to trust him with the truth. He had a wicked tongue, and she couldn't tell yet whether he was nasty or nice. "Why don't you grab one of those saddles from the rail there?" she said. "Take a blanket and bridle, and we'll saddle up some horses for the next trail ride. Mr. Dodge's only got two wranglers left, and today one of them's out with a party and the other's gone on an emergency."

"For all I care, Dodge can saddle his own horses." Ryan's arms stayed folded.

"Don't you like horses?"

"I don't know any personally." His lip twitched as if he were holding back a grin.

"But you said you'd ridden."

"I didn't say I *liked* the experience."

A dimple appeared in each cheek as his smile broke loose. He was good-looking in a dark, heavy way, Lainey decided, but she had nothing in common with this boy, nothing at all. "If you don't want to learn and you won't work, I guess I can't make you," she said, letting her disappointment show.

He snorted. "No, you can't."

So there went her free riding time! She jerked a light-weight saddle off the railing and lugged it to the corral, abandoning Ryan abruptly.

Lady was in her usual place in the partial shade of the mesquite whose lower branches had been chewed off by the horses. The mare turned her mild brown eyes to watch Lainey approach. She took the bit without a fuss as Lainey told her, "You're such a good girl, aren't you, Lady? I hope they give you a gentle rider who treats you right today."

Saddling a cooperative horse like Lady took only a couple of minutes. Lainey went back to the stable for another saddle. Probably Shiloh, who was tall but well behaved, would go in this group, too.

"Mr. Dodge," Lainey called, catching sight of him coming out of the ranch house, "how many do you want saddled?"

"Six. For a bunch of kids. See you already did Lady. We'll send Andy and Buckaroo, Shiloh and Chester. Sugar, too, maybe. Where's Ryan?"

"In the barn. I don't think he feels like working."

"That so?"

"Ummm," Lainey said. She figured it wasn't her business to tell Mr. Dodge that Ryan wouldn't cooperate.

She went about saddling Buckaroo and then Sugar,

the palomino that all the little girls wanted to ride. It didn't seem to bother them that the horse spooked at every piece of litter on the road and was likely to throw them if they didn't stay alert.

Lainey was ready for her fourth horse when Mr. Dodge came out of the stable behind her with a saddle, a big heavy one, and the bridle with the high curved bit they used on Whiskey to try and make him behave.

"Did you talk to Ryan?" she asked.

"His dad oughta've known better than to start remaking a half-grown boy right off." Mr. Dodge scrunched up his lips and nodded to himself. "Can't blame the boy for being madder than a horse with a burr under his saddle. I told him he could work or not as he pleased. It's up to him."

"So I guess I don't get any free rides," she said.

"Who says? You're helping me, aren't you? You can ride free today and tomorrow, Lainey. Can't expect you to train a kid that don't want to be trained."

Mr. Dodge hauled the saddle over to Chester. The big red clown of a horse was busy demolishing the fence.

"Is that horse hungry or something?" The voice was Ryan's. He'd come out from the barn and was standing behind Lainey.

"Chester's a chewer," she said. "Whenever he gets bored he chews on the fence. He's a little foolish, but he behaves himself if you let him follow the leader on a trail ride."

"You know all these horses?"

"There's only thirty. Sure, I know them. I've been riding here for years, and most of the horses have been here longer than me."

"Listen," Ryan said, "I'm here, too, and I don't have a book with me, so if you want to teach me how to saddle a horse, I might as well learn."

Lainey gave him a long look without saying anything. He shrugged and said, "I'm sorry I gave you a hard time. It's not your fault my father's a turkey. Look, this is your territory. You're the boss."

"Fine," she said. "Want to do Andy, that little bay over there? He's pretty easy."

"You do it, and I'll watch," Ryan said.

When Lainey put the bit in the bay's mouth, Ryan's lip lifted and his brows lowered in disgust or disbelief. His expression was so comical she almost laughed. "What's wrong?" she asked.

"Do you have to stick your fingers in their mouths? There must be a safer way to make them take the bit."

"They're used to it, Ryan. You won't lose any fingers, trust me."

"Listen, my fingers have to be tastier than fence rails, and if a horse will chew on those—"

"By tomorrow it'll seem natural to you," she said, wondering if fear had caused some of his resistance to learning about horses. She tossed the saddle over Andy's back and leaned under his belly to grab the cinch.

"Tomorrow I won't be here. Tonight I'm telling my

father what I came out here for, and if he's not interested, he can send me home."

"To your mother?"

"Yeah. . . . I like my mother. Anything wrong with that?"

"Nothing," Lainey said. "I like my mother, too, but it took two parents to make me. I want to know them both."

"Right," he said. "Exactly my point."

"But you're not giving your father a chance if you go right back home just because he didn't open up the minute you arrived," Lainey said, sounding in her own ears like her mother again. "He's not a book you can pick up and read anytime you want."

Ryan stared at her and said, "Yeah, and you can't tell a book by its cover."

"Are you making fun of me again?" she asked.

"No. Actually, I'm mocking myself for expecting you to be a featherweight because you're little and pretty. . . . Sorry," he said.

His compliment confused her into silence. Why had he said she was pretty when she'd looked in the mirror a thousand times and never seen it? Dad said she was pretty, but that was because she was his only daughter and because of her hair.

Lainey nudged Shiloh away from the feeding rack, slid the bit between his lips, and adjusted the curb strap under his chin. "Shiloh here needs a little more head control," she said keeping her eyes on the horse, "but he's not that difficult. The only really difficult horse here is Whiskey." She pointed to the muscular young animal standing alone at the far end of the corral, whisking his tail at flies. "He hurt a rider this morning."

As if to show her *he* could be difficult when he wanted, Shiloh began backing away from her. Ryan jumped sideways. "Don't worry; Shiloh's okay," she said. "He probably just doesn't feel like going for a ride right now, do you, Shiloh? Hmm?"

Shiloh tossed his head and took a step toward Ryan, who backed even farther away. "You're not afraid of horses, are you?" Lainey asked him.

"I respect anything that can break my foot by stepping on it," Ryan said. "You think that's chicken?"

"No," she said. "But really, there's nothing scary about horses except that they're big."

Just then Whiskey whinnied and reared. He came down on his front hooves and raced the length of the corral. When he reached the fence, he whirled and raced back through a bunch of horses who scattered to get out of his way. He kept galloping straight for Lainey and Ryan. Ryan dove under the railing and out of the corral. Lainey took hold of Shiloh's mane and sprang high onto his bare back just as Whiskey pounded past her feet. He made a sharp turn and galloped back to where he'd started.

"That horse is crazy!" Ryan said.

"He's got a lot of spirit," Lainey said from her head-down position across Shiloh's back.

Ryan frowned at her as if she might be crazy, too.

4

Lainey stepped into the kitchen in time to take Amber's call before the answering machine did. "So how'd you make out at Dodge's?" Amber asked.

"Well, I got a job but not a paying one."

"What good'll that do you?"

Lainey explained.

"You're going to be spending all your time with a boy from New York City?" Amber yelped. "What about me?"

"Not all my time, Amber."

"Listen, I got it worked out. Forget the kid at Dodge's." Amber sounded definite as usual. "I talked to my dad, and he'll rent us a horse for you to use this summer so we can go riding together."

"No!" Lainey said sharply. Then more mildly she added, "No thanks, Amber. I can't do that."

"Why not? It'll be your birthday present. Besides, you're my friend, and I want you riding with me."

Lainey shook her head, stuck for words that would explain that the present was too big and somehow embarrassing. "I can't, Amber. I'm sorry."

"Well, all right for you, Lainey Cobb. I'm mad at you now. Really mad." Bang went the receiver.

Lainey sighed. Eventually, she'd have to try and soothe Amber's hurt feelings, but not now. Especially since she wasn't going to give in about letting Amber's father provide her with the horse her own father couldn't afford.

Mom came in through the front door. She was pink cheeked and perspiring from her short walk home through the heat of the late afternoon sun. "Hi, Lainey. How'd your day go?"

"Not bad." Again Lainey explained about the free riding time at Dodge's.

"Sounds fine," Mom said, "but be careful what you say about it to your father. Don't let on you had to get a job because of him. Understand?"

"I understand."

"You're a good girl," Mom said. The mild compliment pleased Lainey. Dad always made it clear that she was everything he wanted in a daughter, but Mom's approval was rare.

Mom bent down to get out the big pot for pasta. "Fettuccine or thin spaghetti tonight?" she asked Lainey.

"I don't care." Mom raised an eyebrow at her. "Fettuccine," Lainey said to please her.

Mom nodded. "You're not still mad at him, are you?"

Lainey shrugged. "I guess not." It was hard to stay angry at Dad. Hadn't he been her willing horse when she was little, galloping around the house with her on his back yelling at him to giddiap? Hadn't he taken her on camp-outs in the mountains?

She'd never forget sitting within the glowing circle of the campfire and his protective strength, awed by the star-specked black of space that reached out and away forever around them. Daddy was her special person, the one she loved best. Still, he shouldn't have let her wake up on her birthday to take the cold drop and hard landing of finding out she didn't have a horse.

After Dad called to tell them he was coming home late and not to wait for him, Mom served the fettuccine with the cold bean salad she knew Lainey liked. "Eat some of your birthday cake," Mom urged.

Lainey ate without much appetite, even though the cake was a rich, moist chocolate. "It's delicious, Mom," Lainey said.

"Your brothers always liked that recipe best," Mom said. "I would have made your favorite if I'd known what it was."

"I guess I don't have a favorite." Quickly, Lainey added, "Everything you bake is good," but Mom's clear blue eyes doubted Lainey really meant that.

It was nearly ten when Dad walked into the kitchen looking tired and dirty. As he was washing up, the phone rang. The middle child, Peter the musician, was having trouble in New York and needed help—translation, another sizable loan. That sent the parents off for a private talk before Lainey exchanged more than a hug with her father.

While she waited for them to come out of their bedroom she got into the tub to soak and think. There had to be some way to earn money if she could just stretch her imagination a little. She wondered if anyone in the few houses within walking distance needed help cleaning. Even scrubbing sinks and toilets would be better than sitting for little kids who wouldn't listen when she told them not to climb on the kitchen counter. But the dusty, makeshift homes tucked back from the road behind a chicken wire fence or hedge or overgrown prickly pear cactus weren't promising. She'd probably end up donating her services if she found anyone frail enough to need her.

It would be much more fun to work at the ranch. If only there were some paying job like—she thought of Whiskey and how she'd unsaddled him after his bad experience. He could use more attention than the wranglers gave him. But Mr. Dodge wouldn't pay her for that.

Her mind slid off to Ryan. He'd been difficult to deal with, but attractive anyway. Why? Maybe it was just that he was male and, like Mom, she'd always been partial to males. Ever since kindergarten she'd fixed on some especially gutsy or honest or bold boy to yearn after. Not that she ever let any boy know she liked him, and none she liked had ever yet shown an interest in her. Maybe Ryan appealed to her because he was a big guy, like Dad and her brothers. Only Dad had a lighthearted nature while Ryan was pure sludge—except when he smiled.

Imagine him reading on vacation instead of spending every possible minute outdoors! Imagine not being turned on by the whipped cream peaks and folds of mountains stubbled with green after the winter rains. Imagine not hurrying to catch the remnants of sunset-colored clouds before they disappeared into night. Or not being happy to rock in a saddle to a horse's gait as it clip-clopped through the desert while a hawk sailed overhead. Ryan was an oddball, all right. Still, she felt sorry for him. It would be sad not to know your own father.

When she finally got out of the bathtub, her parents still hadn't come out of their bedroom. Some birthday, she thought as she climbed into bed. Becoming a teen-ager better not mean Dad was going to ignore her from now on.

Lainey woke up to a dawn bird chorus feeling cheerful as usual after a good night's sleep. So cheerful that when she caught her father alone at the breakfast table, she could say easily, "Daddy, I'm sorry I gave you a hard time yesterday. I understand about the money."

His eyes were clouded with apology as they met hers. He reached out to stroke the loose cascade of hair she'd brushed a hundred times just for him. "It's not like I meant to disappoint you, Lainey," he said. "I wanted to get you a horse."

"I know. You just should have told me sooner. I mean, I'd have understood if you'd leveled with me."

"What do you mean, leveled?" he said, withdrawing his hand in quick offense. "I'm not hiding anything. I haven't done anything wrong. It's just bad luck that I started a business at the wrong time, that's all."

"I know, Daddy."

"Then what do you mean, leveled?"

"I just mean you can tell me how things are. I'm not a baby. I can take it."

"Yeah, well, we're not out in the street yet. I may not be doing for you what your friend Amber's dad does for her, but I will. We'll pull out of this, and you'll see. I'll come through for you. I'll come through for the whole family." He slammed his hand on the table so hard that the mourning dove salt and pepper shakers jumped. His anger startled her.

"I'm sorry, Daddy. I'm sorry." She put her arms around him in an effort to calm him down. He felt as nerved up as Whiskey had been after that man abused him.

Dad patted her back. "It's okay, honey. I know. I'm just—don't mind me, okay? . . . So how did you enjoy your birthday ride yesterday?"

"I didn't take one. I'm going to save the money you gave me."

"What for?"

"So I can buy my own horse." She said it proudly, expecting him to be impressed with her independence, but he pulled away from her and stood up in one swift motion. His craggy face looked bleak. For the second day in a row he walked out on her without saying good-bye.

She had said the wrong thing again.

"Daddy!" Lainey was pressing her fingers to her lips when Mom appeared. She had been in the bathroom and missed the whole discussion.

"Did you speak to your father?" Mom asked.

Lainey nodded.

"Well, good." Mom yawned and slid her bulky body onto one of the tall stools at the kitchen counter. She poured herself a cup of coffee.

"It wasn't good. Dad's acting crazy," Lainey burst out.

"Oh-oh! Well, don't take it to heart. It's not you, Lainey. The bank told him yesterday that if we can't make the next payment, they're going to foreclose on this property."

"Mom!"

"Right. We're in a tight squeeze. And having to find a couple more thousand for Peter doesn't help relieve your father's anxiety. We need to go easy on him." She gave Lainey half a smile. "See what you get for growing up? An earful of your parents' troubles. . . . Or would you rather I keep them from you like I used to?"

"Uh-uh," Lainey said. "I want to know what's going on in my own family."

"Fine, just don't *you* take to worrying, though. It's

enough that your father does it. Worrying only makes things seem worse. And it'll probably work out okay. Money troubles usually do."

Lainey nodded. "Think positive."

Mom laughed. It was what she always said when Lainey worried about some test she had to take in school.

Lainey ate toast and cheese and drank a glass of milk, then took off for Dodge's ranch. When she got there, Chick and Lopez were saddling up a long string of horses for an all-day pack ride into the mountains. There was no sign of Ryan.

"Hey, Lainey," Chick called over his shoulder. "Hear you're going to be working with us." His grin lifted his scraggly blond sideburns into his long hair.

"Not hardly," she said. And if Ryan didn't appear she wouldn't have a job at all.

"Just don't get yourself promoted over me. I already got enough bosses with Lopez and Dodge," Chick joked.

"I'm not your boss," Lopez said in his usual unsmiling way. "I'm not anybody's boss."

"Good thing the horses don't know that," Chick teased him. Lopez moved to the next animal and slung a blanket neatly onto its back. He hadn't acknowledged Lainey's presence.

She found Mr. Dodge in his office taking a phone reservation for an eight-year-old's birthday party trail ride. When he was finished, Lainey asked for permission to take Lady out.

"Take any horse you want that's there, honey."

"Ryan's not coming?"

"Haven't heard. Wouldn't surprise me if he was on his way to the airport."

"I bet he isn't," she said. "I bet he wants to get to know his father as much as his father wants to get to know him."

"Maybe so. The kid don't want to be a cowboy, though. That's for sure."

She laughed. Then she threw out the notion that she'd gotten in the bathtub, even though she guessed it was more of a fantasy than a practical idea. "So since I can't train Ryan, how about giving me a chance with Whiskey?"

"How's that?"

"Give me the job of training Whiskey for you. Would you pay me to do that?"

Mr. Dodge put his booted foot up on the desk and leaned back in his desk chair considering. "I'd pay you if you could do it. Thing is Whiskey didn't get trained right as a colt and horses don't retrain easy. . . . If I'd had my wits about me, I'd never have gotten stuck with him. Traded cash and a good old quarterhorse for that ornery, useless hunk of horseflesh."

"What if I could make him useful?"

Mr. Dodge considered some more while she held her breath. Then to Lainey's delight he said slowly, "Well, he's not a mean one. He don't bite or kick. He could throw you, though, Lainey." He poked at a back tooth with his tongue, still thinking. "Tell you what," he said.

"You get your folks to agree in writing that's it's okay with them if I let you work with him, and I'll give you half of whatever more I get for Whiskey than he's worth now. That's if you improve his manners enough so I *get* any more. How's that strike you?"

"Money?" she said. "You'll give me *money* if I can train Whiskey?"

"That's what I'm saying."

"It could even be enough money to let me buy my own horse," Lainey said, thinking out loud.

"Well, I suppose it might be a good chunk of cash. But frankly, I doubt you can do anything with that animal."

"I can try," Lainey said. Her heart beat a joyous tattoo.

She ran out to the corral, which looked empty with half the horses out on the all-day ride. Over near the mesquite tree, Whiskey was rolling in the dirt, his four legs at awkward angles in the air. What a mess he was. She bet no one had brushed or curried him for ages. Eagerly, she went to the barn to get a rag and a brush, a hoof pick and a currycomb, and a halter.

Whiskey was standing up and watching her by the time she approached him.

"So how would you like a good grooming, Whiskey? Want somebody to fuss over you a little?" He dipped his head to her hand, but she hadn't brought any treat for him. Tomorrow she'd start winning him over with carrots or bread or something tasty. "Come on, Whiskey, you and I, we're going to be good friends," she said.

As if he understood her intention, he cooperated when she put the halter on him and led him to the rail outside the barn where she tied him. Telling him what she planned to do at each step of the grooming, she began roughing out the caked dirt and grime on his near side. She wanted him to get accustomed to the sound of her voice, and judging by the alertness of his ears, he was listening to her.

"I know you're not going to just let me get on your back and ride you past your quarter-mile limit just because I give you a little attention, Whiskey. But maybe if you start liking me. Just maybe. . . . Anyway, whatever I do, I don't plan to hurt you. Do you believe me?"

She laid her hand on the smooth slide of his neck. "I'd rather never ride you at all than dig a spur in your side or beat you with a quirt. I'm not going to maul your mouth with that nasty bit either." His big brown eye attended her with interest. "So what do you think, huh? Think I'm going to be a good horse trainer? Or do you think I'm a fool? I realize I don't know much. I mean not like Lopez, but I'll learn, won't I? Hmm?"

Whiskey ducked his head as if he were answering her, and she laughed at herself for half thinking he might be. His throaty sigh sounded as if he were enjoying the currying. She worked on him for over an hour before she put him back in the corral. Now his woodsy hide gleamed red in the sun and his black mane shone. As he stepped with a fluid grace to the feeding station to scrounge a few stray bits of hay from the manger, smooth young muscles worked under his unmarked skin.

He looked like the best horse Mr. Dodge owned, Lainey thought. Why should a quarter of a mile be his limit? Had something happened to him at that point in the road? Had he been scared there? As soon as she got her parents to sign the permission slip Mr. Dodge wanted, she could test to see if it was just that particular place that Whiskey wouldn't pass.

Meanwhile, she had a free ride coming to her, and why not take it? Lady was gone, but Badger had been left behind this morning. He was fat and old, but sweet tempered. She saddled him and rode him down the road past her own house and up into the mountains. Beside the canyon trail she was following, a spring still trickled into a pool of water on a wide rock basin by the white branches of a dead sycamore. It was late enough in the morning so that she felt as if she were moving through a sauna bath except in the shade of the rocks. A lizard skittered across her path. A hawk circled high against the dense blue sky.

Mr. Dodge said it was hard to retrain a horse, Lainey thought, and Chick had told her once that horses were brainless. He had said even Lopez believed that. But Whiskey seemed so intelligent—the way he took notice of her, his alertness. And some horses had to be smarter than others. At least, they certainly had different quirks and habits.

Chester chewed on things. Lopez's horse bit other horses when they crowded him. Lady preferred her spot under the mesquite tree to the shade of the shed roof where the other horses rested. Didn't having a preference show intelligence? And if Whiskey was intelligent, he could change. He could learn that a long walk into the mountains was more fun than being in a mucky corral all the time.

Swaying comfortably in the saddle as Badger plodded along, Lainey thought how exciting, how wonderful, how fantastic it would be if she could train Whiskey to be as good as he looked. It would be great for her and better for him, too. First, though, she had to convince her father that it was safe for her to train a horse nobody else could deal with.

She thought regretfully about their breakfast conversation. He didn't like the idea of her buying her own horse. Well, if he wasn't able to bring down the moon when she asked for it, he should at least be willing to let her try for it herself.

5

*D*ad strode into the kitchen that evening, head up and grinning. "Spoke to the bank," he told Mom. "Looks like they'll give us a little leeway after all."

"There," Mom said. "Didn't I tell you you could talk the spots off a leopard if you set your mind to it, Randall?"

"I said a *little* leeway," Dad said. "We still need to get some serious buyers around here."

"Well, a young couple came asking about the model houses today. Could be our luck's about to turn." Mom bent to baste the roasting chicken.

The spicy scent of the chicken blended with the heady aroma of optimism in the room. The time was right to get their signatures for Mr. Dodge, Lainey figured. She set the table, laying the permission slip she'd typed and a pen beside Dad's plate.

"What's this?" he wanted to know when he came back from washing up and sat down to eat.

"It's for Mr. Dodge," Lainey said. "No big deal. He just doesn't want to be blamed if I fall off a horse or something like that."

Dad read the sentence which she had paraphrased for him and picked up the pen, but then he hesitated. "How come Dodge is getting fussy about liability all of a sudden?"

"Oh, because a man broke his leg this week. It was his own stupid fault, but Mr. Dodge is afraid he might sue. He worries about everything since his wife died."

"Dodge is getting pretty old," Dad said. "Must be up in his seventies." His fingers did the flourish in the air he performed before he signed anything important, and he bunched his broad shoulders to the task.

Lainey was about to let out her breath when Mom asked, "Is something different about the riding you're going to do now? Is that why Mr. Dodge wants a permission slip?" Mom had put on her glasses and was standing behind Dad reading the one line Lainey had typed. Lainey clenched her teeth. With glasses or without, Mom was sharp-eyed.

"It's just that I'm training this particular horse," Lainey explained casually. "If I train him well, I'll get part of the profit when Mr. Dodge sells him. I'm hoping it will be enough so I can buy my own horse."

Dad winced but Mom said, "Well, aren't you the enterprising one!"

"I guess it runs in the family," Lainey said, nudging Dad's arm.

Dad ignored the flattery and asked, "Why does this particular horse need training?"

"Just because Whiskey's got a bad habit."

"Such as?"

Lainey squirmed a little before explaining casually, "He turns around and goes back to the ranch before he's supposed to. He's not mean or anything, just stubborn."

"You mean you're going to ride him and try to force him to keep going?" Dad asked. "Is that it?" He put down the pen decisively.

"There's no danger. I'm not going to get hurt," Lainey hastened to assure him. "Whiskey's a good horse. Really. He just needs more attention than the wranglers have time to give him."

"Lainey," Dad said, "I know how bad you want a horse, but I won't have you risking your neck for one."

"You let my brothers go rock climbing and motorcycle racing, didn't you?" she demanded.

"They're boys. You're a girl."

"So I'm a girl. I'm as good at riding as they were at climbing or racing."

"Boys are different," Dad said. "A boy needs to learn to take risks. Girls grow up to get married and raise babies. They don't—" He ran out of words under Lainey's glare. "Connie, you tell her," he begged.

"I don't know." Mom's lower lip rolled out as she considered, and Lainey held her breath. At least *Mom* could be trusted not to let emotions rule her judgment. Lainey was jubilant when Mom finally said, "You never know what a woman might have to deal with, Randall. And Lainey's not reckless. As long as this horse isn't mean—"

"He's not, Mom. He's just stubborn. Really. And the minute it looks like I can't handle him, I'll give it up, I promise. Is it all right with you, then?"

Mom nodded. "So long as you're really careful."

Lainey turned to her father. She expected he'd give in easily now that she had Mom's support, but instead he said, "Well, it's not all right with me."

He banged his chair back from the table, making Mom wince as his heavy work boots came down hard on the brittle Mexican tiles. "What if she gets knocked off and a thousand pounds of horseflesh falls on top of her?" he asked Mom. "What if she injures her head, or—no. No way. I want my pretty little girl to stay pretty." Dad's lips curved down in a firm negative.

"Is *that* all you think I am, Dad? Just pretty and little?" Scorn singed Lainey's voice. "Pretty and little— any fool can be that."

"Now, now," Dad said. "Don't get mad, honey. I'm not insulting you. I'm just saying—"

"You *are* insulting me," she shouted in a fit of temper that had been building ever since Dad hadn't trusted her enough to tell her the truth about her birthday present. "I'm tougher than you think, and I can do plenty of things that don't have anything to do with my being a girl."

"Hey, now." Dad reached out a hand toward her. "Take it easy, honey baby. I'm glad you're a girl. When you were born, you should have heard me crowing to everybody about what a sweet, cute little daughter we got." He stopped and looked at his wife pleadingly, as if he realized he'd said the wrong thing again.

Lainey was furious. Every muscle in her clenched, and she had an urge to do something violent. Dad smashed things when he got mad. Mom turned to ice. What Lainey did was jump up from the table and race down the hall to her bedroom.

There she was in the mirror above her dresser, the way her father saw her—a smallish figure of a girl with an oval face, a nothing nose, and hair that flowed luxuriantly over her shoulders down to her waist. That hair! It took as much trouble to keep it shining and smooth as it took to groom Whiskey. And it was hot having long hair in the summer. "I hate it," she said to her mirror image. "I hate the way it makes me look."

She grabbed a handful of hair on either side of her face and pulled it back. Without the hair to advertise her femininity, she looked more competent and capable. More like a boy, Dad would say. How could he be so old-fashioned? He'd swear he considered women the equal of men, "and more," he'd protest, boasting about his wife's business sense and bookkeeping skills. But the truth was he saw women as the weaker sex—not as physically strong, not as brave, not as daring. Pretty and little! Kittens were pretty and little, and baby chicks. It was maddening.

Lainey marched to the hall closet and took out a pair of sharp scissors from Mom's sewing box. Then she locked herself in the main bathroom, even though she had it all to herself since her brothers had gone. Standing in front of the sink on tiptoe, she began lopping off long swatches of hair. When she finished, her hair hung chin length on either side of her face, a little longer in back. And she looked plainer—not so female. Maybe now her father could begin to respect her.

Her heart was pounding. To calm herself, she went back to her bedroom and found the biography of Sally Ride that she'd begun reading for English class this spring. Thinking of Ryan, who could spend a whole vacation on books, she read fifty pages before Amber interrupted her with a phone call.

"You busy tomorrow morning?"

"I may be," Lainey said.

"What do you mean 'may be'? Something to do with that boy?"

"No, Amber. I'm trying to convince my father to let me train a horse for Mr. Dodge."

"*You're* going to train a horse? What do you know about that? You never even had your own horse."

"I've read about it, and I've watched."

"I can't believe Dodge would let you be a trainer. Is he going to pay you for it?"

"Maybe. If I'm successful."

"This I've got to see," Amber scoffed. "Is it a colt or a filly?"

"A grown horse with a bad habit. It's Whiskey."

"*Whiskey?* You're going to train *that* outlaw? You've got to be kidding, Lainey."

"Amber," Lainey said, "you're supposed to be my friend. What are you my friend for if you think I'm such a dud?"

"Sheesh," Amber said. "I'll talk to you when you're in a better mood." As usual, she hung up without a good-bye.

Amber got more blunt and tactless all the time, Lainey thought irritably as she set the receiver back on the hook. If they didn't see each other for a while, that would suit Lainey just fine. She drew her feet up under her and went back to her book.

In the morning, Dad's expressive eyes widened in horror when he saw her hair. "Why'd you have to go and do that, Lainey?" he cried. His face creased as if he were in pain. "Never mind telling me. I know," he said, and without another word he signed the paper that was still lying at his place at the table.

Mom said the hair looked fine. "It'll be cool for the summer. And it'll grow," she added. Lainey couldn't tell if the comfort was meant for Dad or her. After Mom also signed the paper, she said, "You just better take care you don't get hurt now."

"I'll be careful, really, Mom. And thanks."

Lainey put her hand on her father's sleeve to thank him, too, but he wouldn't look at her. He wouldn't speak to her either. She'd hurt him again, and it hurt her that she had. She hoped training Whiskey would be worth all this emotional turmoil in the end.

With the fuss about the permission slip still on her mind, Lainey set off for the ranch, forgetting to bring a treat for Whiskey. She dropped the signed paper on Mr. Dodge's desk, and said, "There you are. I'll start with Whiskey this morning."

"Well, well, well." Mr. Dodge was eyeing her rather than the paper. "Got a haircut, did you?"

"Yes," she said defiantly. "Do you like it?"

"Oh, a pretty girl's a pretty girl however she does up her hair." Too much of his teeth showed when he smiled. "Be careful with Whiskey, now. Remember Lopez tried to break him when we first got him, and Whiskey reared up and fell over backward. Would've killed Lopez if he hadn't jumped free in time. That horse starts rearing, you stop trying to make him do whatever you're trying to make him do. Just stop cold, hear?"

"Yes," Lainey said. "I hear."

"Okay, then. Go to it."

She paused in the doorway of the office to ask, "Did Ryan go back East, do you know?"

"No. He's still in town. His dad claims he told Ryan he could laze around the house all day if he liked, but not to expect him to stay home from work to keep him company. Funny kid, that Ryan."

Lainey nodded. "He likes to read. He won't mind being alone all day." And it wasn't likely he'd get bored and come back to the ranch, she thought regretfully. No, it wasn't likely she'd see him again.

6

W hiskey was in a crowd of horses near the manger, which had just been filled with hay.
Lainey set a saddle and blanket outside the barn and
carried a bridle to him in the corral. "Whiskey," she
called. Then she whistled two notes that she hoped he'd
learn to recognize as his. "Whiskey, want to go for a
ride?"

She began by stroking him as he ate. Then she looped
the reins over his neck, talking to him all the while.
"This morning we're going for a nice ride, just you and
me. It'll be fun, Whiskey. Give you a chance to stretch
your legs out. You don't want to spend all your time in
this corral, do you? Of course you don't. You need your
exercise."

His head was turned back so he could eye her as he
chewed his hay. She kept smoothing his hide, which
was the brown of a tilled field in spring, and talking
until he had eaten his fill. Then she held the leather

headstall up with one hand and slipped the bit in his mouth with the other.

He opened his mouth to take the bit, showing big, square teeth in his upper and lower jaw, but he jerked his head and backed away from her. She stayed alongside him, easing the bridle over his ears, as he pushed his way backward into the other horses, who sidestepped out of the way. "There," she said. "Now that wasn't so bad, was it?"

Still moving slowly and talking to him, she led him out of the corral, being careful to shut the gate behind her. At the hitching rail outside the barn, she flipped the saddle blanket onto his back and heaved the light saddle she'd chosen neatly on top of it. A quick duck under his belly and she grasped the cinch, which she tightened snugly. It pleased her that at least Whiskey would let her saddle him. So far so good. He still had his head turned so he could see her. His ears twitched back and forth, but he didn't have the mean look of a horse that intends to bite.

"You're just interested, aren't you?" she asked him. "Just want to know what I'm planning to do. Well," she said, "what we're going to do is try riding along the road to the right instead of left. That way you can't tell when you've gone a quarter of a mile because we won't be walking past my house, see? And if it was something there that scared you, well, we won't be passing it. So what do you think? Think I'm smart to figure that out, huh?"

She put her foot in the stirrup and lifted herself

lightly into the saddle. Whiskey stood still as he was supposed to and snuffled softly. She smiled to herself. What if he behaved for her? What if he acted like a perfectly trained horse in her hands? That would be wonderful in one way, but not so wonderful in another because Mr. Dodge wouldn't owe her anything if she couldn't prove she'd trained Whiskey. She clucked and directed the horse toward the road. The light touch of her heels against his ribs was enough to get him walking.

Lopez was leading a lame horse to the barn. He turned to ask, "What are you doing on Whiskey, girl?" The sun glinted off the silver in the triangular beard he was growing. It made him look like a Spanish conquistador straight out of a social studies book.

"Mr. Dodge gave me permission to train him," Lainey said. "I'm going to ride him down the road to the right. Did you try him in that direction, Lopez?"

He nodded. "Whiskey's limit's the same both ways."

She was disappointed, "Well, what should I try, then?" she asked.

Half his thin mouth lifted in a smile. "Try riding another horse," he said and continued on his way to the barn.

She sat up straighter. So what if Lopez didn't think she could do it. He might know horses, but he'd tried and failed with this one. Whiskey was different, and it was just a matter of figuring out how.

Whiskey turned calmly to the pressure of knee and rein and walked along the road to the right even though it was an unusual direction for him. There were no riding trails that way. He seemed so accepting of Lainey's control that she even risked stopping him so that she could adjust her left stirrup. She'd been too anxious when she mounted to notice it was a little short.

"Come on, Whiskey, you're doing great, boy." She nudged him in the ribs with her heels to get him started again. He walked so sedately that she could relax and notice a late-blooming cholla whose startling red flower hadn't completely faded yet. The morning sun massaged her shoulders gently. Only an occasional commuter vehicle to Tucson sped past, kicking up loose gravel at Whiskey's legs.

"Isn't this fun?" she asked him. "Aren't we having a good time? And if you're real good, I'll give you some oats when we get back to the corral." Oats were a special treat. Mr. Dodge didn't dole them out unless a horse was off its feed for some reason.

When they got as far as the hotel—that would be a mile—she would turn around, because riding on the shoulder of the road wasn't all that much fun. She would walk Whiskey back past the stable and—

In the middle of her thought, Whiskey began turning.

"Hey, what are you doing?" She pulled the reins against his turn. Ignoring the pressure of reins and her knees, he kept going until he was facing back the way they'd come. A quarter of a mile, she realized, that's what he had done. That's what he would do—no more. He wasn't obeying her at all. He was doing what he wanted to do.

"Oh, no you don't," she said, and insisted with the

rein and her legs that he turn back to go toward the hotel.

Whiskey tossed his head to get rid of the pressure of the high arched bit in his mouth. He snorted and tossed his head again, moving in the direction she wanted. But he continued in a circle right into the middle of the road and swung around until he was heading back to the ranch.

"Whiskey, you stop that now." She fought him until he broke out in a surge of power and galloped for home.

Standing in the stirrups on the runaway horse, with one hand grasping the reins and the other clutching the saddle horn, Lainey felt as if she were on the edge of a diving board and about to fall off. Holding the horn also put her out of sync with the wild rhythm of Whiskey's gallop. Neither reins nor horn was firm enough to keep her from flying off Whiskey's back. One unexpected jerk and she'd be thrown onto the roadway. It took all her willpower to squeeze her fear into a hard little ball, let go of the horn, and pull back on the reins with both hands.

"Whoa, Whiskey. Slow down. You can't gallop on this highway. It's against the law." Her shoulders ached, but she kept sawing on the reins. Finally, he slowed into a fast trot the last hundred feet to the ranch. To Lainey's dismay, as she came bouncing in, Lopez just happened to be on horseback near the corral. He was talking to Chick, who had come back from leading the sunrise trail ride.

With a big grin, Chick opened the latch on the corral

gate for her. He bowed mockingly and said, "Here she is, the horse trainer. How'd you do, Lainey?"

"Well, I kept Whiskey from galloping all the way back," she said.

"No kidding! Guess you showed him who was boss, huh?"

Lainey bit her lip, refusing to respond to his mockery, but she couldn't keep her face from flushing.

"Face it, kid," Chick said. "That horse won't give in lessen you can beat him to his knees or starve him, and you haven't got the guts for that."

"I don't think breaking a horse's spirit is the way to tame him," Lainey said.

"You don't, huh? What do you think of that, Lopez? Think this girl knows something we don't know?" Chick was leaning toward Lopez as if hanging on his answer.

"I think Whiskey's the wrong horse for you, Lainey," Lopez said.

It surprised her that he had used her name, and it pleased her that at least *he* wasn't making fun of her. "Well, I'm not finished with him yet," she said. She ignored the opened corral gate and rode Whiskey to the barn, where she tied him to the hitching rail.

Out of the corner of her eye she saw Lopez enter the corral and ride toward the fence at the far end with Chick following him on foot. Both men were carrying tools to repair the fence. Lainey was relieved that they'd turned their attention away from her.

For a few minutes she stood stroking Whiskey to calm him, although he seemed calm enough now that they were back. Then she brought him a bucket of oats from the feed bin in the barn. "There you go, fella. I know you don't deserve it yet, but maybe if I'm nice to you, you'll want to be nice to me, huh?"

When he was finished eating, she mounted him again. This time they went in the usual direction, to the left.

As soon as she saw Cobb Lane Development coming into view, she started talking to Whiskey, telling him what a basically fine horse he was, "and so beautiful," she said. His ears turned back to listen. She talked with more animation, hoping to keep him distracted enough so he'd forget to turn around.

To her dismay, he began turning just before they got to Cobb Lane's arch. Patiently, she allowed his turn as if it were her idea, but then she tugged him past the direction he'd meant to go and back the way they'd been heading in another 360-degree circle.

She dug her heels in and said, "Okay, Whiskey, let's go."

He reared and neighed and reared again. A bolt of fear split her gut as she remembered Mr. Dodge's warning. If the horse got desperate enough, he'd rear so high he'd fall backward, hurting either or both of them.

A station wagon passed her. Children's faces stared out the back window, goggle-eyed, as Whiskey did his Wild West act.

In any case, fighting her wasn't what she wanted Whiskey to remember. She gave him his head, and they loped back toward the ranch. Again she managed to slow him enough so they were trotting rather than galloping when they turned in the driveway.

This time, after she tied him to the rail outside the barn, she removed his saddle. Then she went for the currycomb and brush and rags. She worked out her frustration grooming Whiskey, starting with the hot, sticky side of his neck and working back toward his haunches.

"How come you're being so good to a cuss that done you wrong?" Chick asked. He rested the sole of his pointy, tooled-leather cowboy boot on the hitching rail.

"Just feel like it," she said.

"Don't make sense to reward a horse for bad behavior," Chick said.

"So what would you do to teach him?"

"Like I told you. Tie him up, don't give him any food or drink, use the quirt hard on him, and get yourself some spurs to dig in his hide."

She swallowed. He was dead serious. "I couldn't do that to an animal," she said. Chick guffawed. Lopez, who was passing them on foot this time, raised an eyebrow and said nothing.

"Anyway, it won't hurt to try training him my way, will it, Lopez?" Lainey asked.

"No," Lopez admitted. "Just cost Mr. Dodge some oats."

Chick acted as if that was the funniest thing he'd heard in a week. He reminded her of her brothers, who had enjoyed teasing her if they noticed her at all, and she was glad when he and Lopez walked on past her into the barn. It was lunchtime. They were going inside to eat.

She kept roughing up Whiskey's dark matted hair and then using the brush to smooth it. He whisked his long black tail at the flies that had gathered and muttered to himself contentedly. When she was done, she rubbed him shiny with a rag.

"Tomorrow," she told him, "I'll bring you some bread. Think you'd like that? Hmmm, Whiskey?"

The intelligent brown eye with its fringe of black lashes regarded her with interest. A surge of liking for the independent animal filled her throat. Why should he obey any two-footed stranger who came along? Why shouldn't he have a will of his own? "You want to be respected, don't you, Whiskey?" she whispered. "Well, I can understand that all right. Yes, I can."

As if he understood, Whiskey nudged her with his head. He was saying thank you, Lainey thought, and she smiled.

7

Two days of getting the silent treatment from her father was all Lainey could stand. The second night when he came home with sawdust in his hair from the carpentry work he'd been doing and grunted in answer to her greeting, she went into action. She wrapped her arms tight around him and said, "Daddy, I'm not letting you go until you forgive me for cutting my hair and whatever else you're mad at me for."

"I'm not mad at you, Lainey."

"Yes you are. You won't talk to me."

He took a deep breath and said without meeting her eyes, "I just don't much feel like talking these days."

"Then smile at me, at least, so I know you're not mad."

He gave her a smile so sad it pained her. "You doing okay with the horse?" he thought to ask.

"I don't know," she said. "I'm trying."

He nodded. "Well, let's hope you have better luck than your father's having."

It was a comfort to know she wasn't the main cause of his blue funk, but she blamed herself for some of it anyhow. When Lainey had asked her why she and her father were having such a hard time getting along lately, Mom had said, "Your father just doesn't like the idea of you growing up." But she had to grow up, didn't she? Was she supposed not to try being independent because it pained him when he was already hurting? She hadn't come up with an answer to that yet. She only knew that being a good daughter was not as easy as it had been when she was little.

The third time that Lainey arrived with a couple of slices of dry bread and whistled for Whiskey, he actually left the company of two other horses to saunter across the corral to her.

"Good boy, Whiskey," she told him with delight. "You're beginning to know me, aren't you?" She fed him the bread with one hand and stroked him with the other.

"Nice-looking horse," a male voice said behind her.

She turned to see who belonged to it. "Ryan! What are you doing here?"

"Came to do some riding."

"Oh. . . . Not to work?"

"Me, work?" He mimicked horror. Then he grinned

and said, "Anyway, not outdoors in this climate. No, my father's planning to take me on a weekend ride to see Indian rock paintings in some canyon. He wants me to get my butt in shape for it. Also, I'm supposed to learn how to care for my own mount so he doesn't have to do it for me."

"You and your father must be getting along, then."

"Well, we're sniffing around each other. How are you doing?"

"Okay."

"I'm sorry I took your job away from you. I mean, training me."

"Oh, that's okay. Mr. Dodge gave me a better deal than earning free rides."

"What's that?"

"I'm training this horse." She patted Whiskey's neck. "When I get him tamed so he can be sold, I'll get part of the profit."

"He looks pretty tame to me."

She smiled, knowing better. "So who are you riding?"

"I don't know. Any suggestions?"

"Ask for Lady maybe, or Shiloh. They're easy to handle and give you a really smooth ride besides."

"Thanks," he said. "I have to find Chick. Dodge says he's the only wrangler around this morning."

"Chick was in the barn last I saw him."

She watched Ryan go. He was easier to talk to than any boy in her school, more like an adult than a kid, and he was likable. But no way could she understand anyone who took pride in being lazy. Dad wouldn't know what to make of him either. Unless Ryan was just striking a pose. That could be, Lainey thought.

She went about the business of saddling Whiskey. "Now this morning, no foolishness. We're going for a real long ride, okay?" she told him.

He stood patiently while she mounted him, which didn't mean a thing, as she knew from experience.

Ryan came back out of the stable lugging a saddle and blanket on one hip and wearing a bridle over his other shoulder.

"Chick claims he's busy," Ryan said. "He says I should get you to help me saddle Chester. Lady and Shiloh are out on the trail with Lopez already. Is Chester a killer?"

"Chester? He's safe, just kind of—" Lainey wrinkled her nose. "Goofy," she finished.

"Sure, just what I'd expect Chick to give me. That guy doesn't even know me and he hates my guts. 'City boy,' he called me."

"He was being polite. He could have called you worse."

Ryan arched an eyebrow and sighed. "Yeah, well, he's taking a group out in half an hour. He said to get Chester ready and walk him around here while I wait. So which is my goofy horse?"

She pointed to the large, angular, reddish brown animal. This morning he was busy gnawing on the manger. "You want to approach him on the left side. That's the side where the horse expects you to be when you're on the ground. They like things to be the way they expect," she said.

"Who doesn't?" Ryan fumbled with the latch on the corral gate, complaining, "These saddles weigh a ton."

"That one's maybe thirty-five or forty pounds," she said. "Mine's lighter because I'm smaller."

"No, really?" Ryan faked amazement.

She bit her lip. He might not like being told the obvious, but she didn't like being mocked for trying to instruct him, either. She was miffed enough not to bother telling him to leave the saddle and blanket outside of the corral so that they wouldn't be dirtied by horse droppings. That, too, was obvious.

It turned out not to be to Ryan, though.

"Now what," he demanded as he stopped next to Chester, who ignored him and kept chewing on the manger.

"Now you put on the bridle."

To get rid of the saddle, Ryan heaved it up on Chester's back. That got the horse's attention! He stopped chewing and jumped sideways. Then he did a quick dance step with his back legs. Ryan jumped out of the way, up against the manger. The saddle fell off Chester, startling him so that he sidestepped fast the other way to avoid the thing that had dropped on the ground beside him. The sight of the horse's great round rump coming at him sent Ryan climbing into the manger. Next he started to scale the fence around the hay stored in the inner ring.

Chick's cackling laugh broke clear above the early

morning birdcalls. He was standing in the barn doorway laughing so hard he was bent double. Now that was mean, Lainey thought. She dismounted, tied Whiskey to the nearest rail, and went to retrieve the bridle that Ryan had dropped in his haste.

"Come on down and I'll show you how to do this, Ryan," she said.

"God, I hate being made a fool of!" he exploded.

"Everyone does," she said calmly. "Come on, now. Hold this bit with your fingers the way I'm showing you, and stand by Chester's head."

Slowly, Ryan descended. He took the bridle stall and held it up. "If this horse bites off my fingers, do I get a medal for bravery or do I get scoffed at again?"

"You get scoffed at, naturally," she said. "Come on. He won't eat your fingers."

Gingerly, Ryan offered Chester the bit, which the horse took as if it were a piece of sugar, barely showing his teeth. "He let me," Ryan said. "Can you believe that? He let me do it."

"Sure. Now slide the crown piece over his ears." Lainey helped him for the sake of Chester's poor ears as Ryan struggled clumsily with the big boxy head. "Next comes the saddle blanket. Be sure it's free of burrs before you put it on."

"Okay, but where does it go?"

"Where do you think? Under the saddle on the horse's back, Ryan."

He frowned at her. "Come on," he said, "don't you give me a hard time, too."

"Why shouldn't I?"

"Because you're a decent kid. Or at least that's how I had you pegged."

She sniffed, pleased enough by the compliment to forgive him for being so smart mouthed. Patiently, she demonstrated how to put on the saddle. By the time Ryan had tightened the cinch and hoisted himself onto the horse, he seemed more confident.

Meanwhile, Chick had saddled a half dozen horses.

"If you try going it alone, City Boy, don't blame me when that old Chester takes off for the next county with you on his back," Chick called in his nasal twang. "You best wait for my group. You'll fit in good with them." He chuckled to himself. A bad sign, Lainey thought.

"I think I'll go with Lainey," Ryan yelled back to him. "Okay?" he asked her, his eyes pleading.

"Suit yourself," Chick said. "But it'll be a real short ride if you go out with Whiskey. He don't go more'n a quarter of a mile." Chick grinned at them both. The bashed-down felt hat he was wearing today made him look tough because it hid his baby face. All you could see of him was hat, long blond hair, and a handlebar mustache that looked fake but wasn't.

"Come on, then," Lainey said to Ryan. She didn't want the distraction of him bumping along on Chester while she was trying to train Whiskey, but she couldn't bring herself to reject Ryan in front of Chick.

She led the way down the road to the left. Once on the gravel verge of the highway, Chester poked his head companionably close alongside Whiskey's haunches.

Since Whiskey didn't seem to object, Lainey allowed Chester to draw abreast, and they walked down the road side by side.

"So how do you like Tucson?" she asked Ryan.

"Not that much," he said. "It's okay at night when it cools down, but baking in a 110-degree oven every day is not my idea of fun."

"Early mornings are nice," she said.

"Early mornings I'm sleeping. Unless I've got a date with a horse. I guess it's what you're used to. . . . Have you always lived here?"

"Always," she said. "I don't mind the summers. And I love the sunshine and mountains in the distance wherever you look. . . . I visited a cousin in upstate New York once. She lives near mountains, the Adirondacks, but they're too green."

"Better too green than the dead brown around here."

"You should see the desert in bloom in the spring. It's full of color then."

"Cacti just don't do it for me," Ryan said. "Give me a nice old maple that I can lean against without getting speared."

She laughed. "So when are you going home?"

"I don't know. I may stick around until I get a handle on what my father's like. . . . He talks to me after dinner usually. He has his coffee, and we sit out on the patio and watch the lizards scarfing up flies, and he talks. There's an owl in a big old tree near the pool. I've never seen an owl in the wild before. We sit there until the stars come out. Then he watches TV and I read some more."

"What does he talk about?"

"Oh, how great he runs the hospital. Or about the West and what Tucson was like when he first came out here. Or what he thinks is going to happen to the old U.S. of A. He's pretty interesting, really."

"What does he think is going to happen to the country?"

"Well, he figures we'll come out on top because we've got what he calls 'vision' and we're natural-born risk takers. Not me, though, I'm not a risk taker." Ryan chuckled. "I guess you could tell by how quick I got out of Chester's way, huh?"

"Chester's pretty big," she said, trying to be fair, "and you're not used to horses."

"Thanks for not laughing at me, Lainey."

"I almost did," she had to admit. "You were pretty funny."

He grinned amiably, showing a dimple in his broad cheek. "I bet I was." Then out of the blue he asked her, "How come you got your hair cut?"

"Why? Don't you like it?"

"Well, sure. I mean, you'd look good anyway, but your hair was special, so long and shiny, kind of like Whiskey's tail. Not that I'm comparing you to a horse. I mean—" He groaned in embarrassment.

To rescue him, she confided, "I cut it off to show my father I'm not his little darling anymore. I'm an individual, and I'm going to grow up and do things because I want to and I can—just like my brothers. You know what I mean?"

"All that from a haircut?" he asked.

She shrugged.

He said, "Well, I guess I can see it. There's a kid in my school who got sent home for having four-letter words shaved onto his head. I guess he was using hair to make a statement, too."

Lainey gave a start. She couldn't believe it. They'd walked past the entrance to Cobb Lane, and Whiskey was still stepping right along. "Ryan, he did it!" she shrieked.

"Who did what?" He looked around in confusion.

"Whiskey." She forced her trembling hands to steady so that Whiskey wouldn't feel her excitement through the reins and start acting up again. "This horse," she practically whispered to Ryan, "always—I mean *always*, no matter who's riding him—turns around and heads for the stable in a quarter of a mile. We've gone at least half a mile already."

"Must be my influence," Ryan said. "Or maybe it's Chester. Hey, Chester, you distracting old Whiskey from his turnaround act?" Ryan leaned slightly forward in the saddle and patted Chester's neck.

Lainey was irked that he wasn't taking this break-through seriously. To her it was amazing that Whiskey had become obedient so suddenly, and for no reason. Unless he was responding to the hours she'd spent grooming him and giving him treats he didn't deserve.

Or did Ryan have it right? Could it be Chester's companionship?

"You know what this means, Ryan? It means I may be able to buy myself a horse soon. At least, I will if Whiskey's broken his bad habit and Mr. Dodge can get a good price for him."

"You want Dodge to sell the horse?" Ryan shook his head as if he were mystified. "I thought you liked Whiskey."

"I do," she said. "But there's no way I can afford him once he's trained. See, then he'll become valuable because he's also young and strong and beautiful."

"So don't tell Dodge you've trained him, and he'll sell Whiskey to you cheap."

"I couldn't do that," she said immediately. "It wouldn't be honest."

Ryan smiled and nodded. "That's what I figured you'd say."

"Would you do it?"

"No," he said.

She gave him one of her mother's level-eyed special looks. He was an oddball, Lainey thought, and not easy to know even if he was an easy talker. Still, she liked him.

They clip-clopped across the road and entered a dirt path, bordered by a rock fence, that led to the state forest trails. A rider came loping toward them. Lainey recognized Amber on Belle. "Amber!" she called out, but her friend pounded on by without a nod or a wave.

"Who's that?" Ryan asked.

"My friend. Or, anyway, she used to be." Lainey looked after Amber in dismay. She'd been too busy to call Amber, and they hadn't seen each other since Lainey's birthday. No wonder Amber didn't want to speak to her.

"I thought it was a boy," Ryan said. "She mad at you or something?"

"Maybe," Lainey said. Then she added hopefully, "Or maybe she didn't realize it was me because I'm with you."

"You mean she doesn't expect to see you with a boy?"

"I guess not."

"Why not?"

"Because . . ."

"Don't you even have a boyfriend in school?"

"No. Do you have a girlfriend?"

"Well, sure. That is, I have friends who are girls. It's no big deal. I mean, it's easier to have a conversation with a girl. Especially the ones that like to read."

She considered what he'd said and decided that she liked his attitude. At least *he* was a male who gave girls credit for concerns beyond their own looks and feelings. She was wishing she were more of a reader herself when suddenly Whiskey started reversing direction.

"Oh, no you don't!" She reined him through the turn and past it, trying to force him back onto the trail. He snorted and began to rear right above a pile of boulders and the barbed spines of a bristling teddy bear cholla. "Whiskey," she said keeping her voice calm to control him, "don't start in now. Look at how far we got. Come on, settle down. Don't you want to see what's up the trail?"

The third time Whiskey rose up on his back legs, neighing as if demanding his release, she heard Ryan cry out her name in terror. It did seem that Whiskey was about to fall backward. Lainey made ready to jump.

When Whiskey came down safely on his front legs, her fear dropped with him. She simply gave him his head and let him gallop for home, leaving Ryan alone on the path behind her. Nearing Cobb Lane, Lainey was afraid her mother might be looking out the window of the trailer, so she tried reining Whiskey in. To her relief, he slowed to a trot.

Chick was coming toward her. He was leading what she had expected—a gaggle of little girls, probably another birthday party group. Into the face of his knowing grin, she said stiffly, "Ryan's back there at the trail head alone."

Chick nodded. "I'll look out for him."

She hoped Ryan wouldn't be humiliated to be stuck with a group of elementary school age girls, but she couldn't do much about it if he was. The best she could manage was to coax Whiskey from a too-fast bouncing trot to a walk.

When she dismounted at the barn, she went as usual to get him his oats and she gave him a thorough grooming. If nothing else, he was looking handsomer from all the attention she had been giving him.

"I treat you a lot better than you treat me, you big trickster," she complained to him. "That wasn't nice, to let me think I had you trained and then show me who's boss. You're too smart for your own good, you know that?"

Playfully, Whiskey bumped her shoulder with his nose.

"Oh, Whiskey, you crazy horse," she said. "Don't you know Mr. Dodge could sell you for dog meat unless you behave?" She put her arms around his neck and hugged him. He kept his head still and snuffled as if her affection pleased him.

Well, she told herself, he had gone past his limit today. What if tomorrow she could get him to go a little farther? What if Chick and Lopez were wrong and Whiskey did get trained her way? For a moment she stood still, embracing Whiskey and hoping for a miracle.

8

*I*t was late Saturday afternoon, and Dad was sprawled on the couch watching the sports channel on TV with a near-empty bottle of bourbon on the cocktail table beside him. He'd been in the same position when Lainey had left for the ranch that morning, but the bottle had been full then. The last time Lainey remembered her father trying to drink away his misery had been on the weekend his oldest son had chosen the air force instead of joining him in the start-up of Cobb Builders.

"Hi, Dad," Lainey said cautiously. "How are you doing?"

He mumbled something without even looking in her direction. She let him be and joined her mother in the kitchen. "What's happened now?" Lainey asked.

"It's just the same old money trouble, Lainey. Nobody's sick or dying."

"But Dad's drinking," Lainey said.

"Well, it discouraged him that the couple who were going to buy a house changed their minds. Don't worry, Lainey. He'll have a hangover tomorrow, and by Monday he'll have revved himself up to try again."

Mom's fair face radiated her usual sunny-day conviction that life was good. She should be a newscaster, Lainey thought. Mom's face would reassure viewers of the world's survival, no matter what awful disasters she was reporting.

Lainey made a bowl of popcorn and silently set it down next to the bottle on the cocktail table. "What's that for?" her father asked.

"For you, Dad."

"I don't want it."

"Want me to bring you a sandwich?"

"I don't want anything. Not hungry." He was dough colored, and his big body looked awkward flung there on the cushions. With his eyes receding into slits and his face puffy, he resembled a beaten boxer.

"I'm sorry, Daddy, about the sale falling through," she offered gently.

His eyes remained fixed on the TV. "So how's it going with the horse?"

"Good. He went past his quarter-mile limit for me yesterday."

"Yeah? Well if you make any money on him, you can lend it to me."

"Okay." She was pretty sure he didn't mean it, but was willing to if he did.

"Because you can forget about getting your own horse," he said. "That's for a rich man's daughter, and you're no rich man's daughter, and never will be the way things are going."

Letting his bitterness bounce off her, she made her voice cheerful and asked, "Dad, would you come over to Dodge's with me so I can show you how Whiskey comes when I call him?"

"I'm not going anywhere today."

"Please, for me, Daddy." Her idea was to lure him away from the bottle and his determination to make himself drunk, but the look he gave her clearly showed he knew what she had in mind.

"Get out of here," he growled. "You stink of horses. Who wants a daughter who stinks of horses?"

That blow found its mark. She ran from the room as if he'd slapped her and went on out to the patio. So he was feeling terrible and she was just a child who couldn't comfort him. But she had feelings, too. He had no right to mock them, not if he cared about her. She stared off into the desert with stinging eyes.

"Lainey," Mom said from the sliding door to the kitchen. "What now? What happened?"

"Nothing."

"If he said something mean, it was just the drink."

"No it wasn't," Lainey said. "He doesn't love me anymore. Maybe he never really did." With an echo of her father's bitterness she added, "How could he when I'm just a girl!"

"Lainey, I don't have the patience to deal with two miserable people at once. Why don't you go visit Amber?"

"She's probably out riding."

"Well, call her. Maybe she isn't."

It was sensible advice. Besides, it was time to make peace with Amber. They'd been friends for four years, and however annoying Amber could be, she had her good qualities. Plus she wasn't just a friend until she could find someone who had more to offer her, like other girls Lainey had known.

Lainey called Amber's private number, and Amber picked up the phone.

"What are you doing?" Lainey asked.

"Hanging out by the pool. What are you doing?"

"Nothing much." Lainey waited for the invitation Amber had never failed to extend. She was proud to share her Olympic-size swimming pool. It was surrounded by cushioned lounge chairs under a thatch-roofed deck that provided shade even on the hottest day. But today Amber said only, "Well, see you around, then."

Lainey gripped the receiver in shock. Amber had hung up on her. Ignoring Lainey on the trail yesterday hadn't been an accident, then. Amber was angry at her, really angry. Was it because they hadn't seen each other in a while? Was their friendship over forever just because of that?

So glum she didn't feel like doing anything at all, Lainey dragged herself to the carport, where she'd left her riding boots. She pulled them on, set her cowboy hat square on her head, and started down the road toward Mr. Dodge's ranch.

The heat of the afternoon sun still weighed heavily on the desert. Not enough air remained to breathe. The horses would all be resting in whatever shade they'd found. Well, she could say hello to Whiskey and chat with Mr. Dodge, or see if anybody was cleaning tack in the barn and offer to help them.

The asphalt at the edges of the road was soft enough to chew. Ahead of Lainey ripples of superheated air made the road look like a gray lake—a lake without water. Inside the heat that was smothering her, the only sounds were the whine of a car speeding by and the creak of her boots.

Suddenly she also heard hoofbeats, and there coming toward her was Whiskey. He was riderless, hooves barely touching the roadway as he galloped freely down the middle of the road. He whipped past her without any sign of recognition, although she called his name and held up the bread she was carrying.

In her dismay, she dropped the bread and ran the rest of the way to the ranch. There she saw Lopez getting into Mr. Dodge's Jeep with a rope in his hand while Mr. Dodge stood under the ramada, worrying his gnarled hands against one another.

"Lainey," he said, "you want to go with Lopez and help him catch that crazy horse of yours?"

Without wasting words, she jumped into the passenger's side of the Jeep. Lopez's skill at handling horses didn't extend to vehicles. He jerked her back in the seat at the start and nearly threw her out the door when he turned too sharply into the road.

"Why did Whiskey take off?" she asked.

"Who knows? First thing I saw was him sailing over the fence. That horse would have made a good jumper if he'd been trained."

"Something must have spooked him."

"With Whiskey you can't ever tell. He does what he pleases. Let's just hope he doesn't run into a truck and kill himself," Lopez said.

It was the dust trail left by Whiskey when he veered off into the wash that alerted them. Lopez muttered *"Madre de Dios"* under his breath and cautiously eased the Jeep down the steep bank onto the dry riverbed. "Easy to get stuck in this sand," he said.

Fortunately, Whiskey hadn't gone very far. They saw him under a mesquite tree, browsing on a growth of green weeds that had taken hold in the dampness there. Lopez stopped the car and stepped out. Coiling the rope, he walked easily toward the horse, who waited until Lopez was within ten feet of him before bolting from his oasis and taking off at top speed farther down the wash. Lopez looked disgusted as he returned to the car.

"Next time, *you* try roping him," he said to Lainey. It thrilled her that Lopez, the expert, would think she might deal with a horse better than he could. She sat up straighter.

They continued along the riverbed with Lopez weaving toward whatever appeared to be solid ground as they went. This time Whiskey had found himself a bank to hide against, and they didn't see him until they turned a sharp bend in the river.

The horse was watching them, ears forward, eyes alert, his dark head held high. Lainey took the coiled rope Lopez handed her. She listened to his instructions on how to use it and slipped out of the car. As she walked slowly toward Whiskey, she gave her two-part whistle.

"I lost the bread I had for you," she told him, "but if you come home with me, I'll get you some oats. What do you say, Whiskey? Want some oats? Or water. I bet you're thirsty, aren't you?"

It was so hot that the sweat had dried in a salty rime on his withers. So hot, Lainey could feel it scorching the back of her shoulders. But the horse seemed immune to the heat. He shifted from one front leg to another and tossed his head at her, nostrils flaring.

"So," she asked, ten feet from him. "You're a good jumper, are you? Sometime maybe we could practice going over hurdles. I always wanted to learn how to ride a jumper. Want to teach me, Whiskey? Hmm?"

She was five feet from him. Any second she expected him to break and run, but now she was close enough to reach out and touch him, and he didn't budge. Even when she looped the rope over his neck to halter him, he stayed put.

"There," she said. "I guess you're ready to go home. Had your fun, didn't you?" She patted the long sleek neck. He bent his head and rested his soft nose on her arm, breathing quietly. "You are something, Whiskey. Playing games like this on such a hot afternoon. Bet you were looking for a swimming hole, weren't you?"

She tugged at the rope facing away from him, and he came with her as she stepped toward the car. He could easily have slid out of the loop she'd made, or yanked the rope out of her hands, but he moved along docilely to within a few feet of the Jeep. There he stopped and snorted, pulling his head back.

"He doesn't like cars. Can you ride him bareback?" Lopez asked.

"I've never tried."

"It's a long way to walk. I'll give you a boost up if you want to try it."

"Sure," she said. Whiskey's trust in her made Lainey feel invincible. She stroked him to keep him calm as Lopez approached. He made his hands into a basket. She stepped into it with her left foot as if it were a stirrup and threw her right leg over Whiskey's bare back. The horse stood obediently still.

Lopez retied the rope around Whiskey's neck into something resembling a hackamore. He gave her the ends of it as reins. "If you get scared, pick a good soft spot and roll off," he said. "I'll drive far enough behind you so I don't spook him."

She nodded. Riding bareback was something she'd done only a couple of times in her life, and that on reliable old horses in friends' fields. Riding Whiskey bareback might be a foolish return of his trust on her part because the sense of mischief that made him interesting also made him dangerous. Probably her parents and Mr. Dodge would consider what she was doing reckless. Well, they weren't around to stop her.

Whiskey walked quietly along the wash toward the road, as if her weight didn't bother him. She turned him with the rein against his neck to get him to climb the bank when they got to where the roadway bridged the riverbed. He let her guide him. Going up the bank, though, Whiskey stumbled and went down on one knee. He recovered, but Lainey lost her balance and slid off him, losing the rope reins in the process.

She scrambled up the slippery bank after him and found him waiting for her at the top. "Oh, you good boy. You good, good boy," she told him, hugging his neck in a burst of affection.

Lopez had gone under the bridge. She heard him gunning the engine on the other side as if he were stuck or else trying to climb the bank.

It made more sense to walk Whiskey back to the ranch from here, Lainey decided, rather than risk riding him bareback on the road, where she could get tossed into the path of a car. Besides, she wasn't sure she could heave herself onto his back without an assist. She began the mile or so hike on the verge of the highway, leading Whiskey by the improvised hackamore. As she was walking past Cobb Lane, Lopez finally drew abreast of her in the Jeep. She grinned because it was the first time she'd ever seen the dapper cowboy looking grungy. He and the Jeep were thoroughly mud splattered.

"It seems you have the instincts to be a good horse trainer," Lopez said, gesturing at Whiskey, who was ambling docilely beside her.

"Thanks." She smiled with pride at the compliment. "Whiskey's a good horse."

"Could be you'll make him into one someday." He took off without further notice from Whiskey, who had stopped to paw at a dead plant he must have thought was edible.

"Come on, you hungry animal. Let's get back and I'll give you some oats," Lainey said happily. Lopez might disapprove of giving Whiskey a reward for bad behavior, but good treatment had inched her close to winning Whiskey's complete trust, and she meant to continue with it.

She even spent a sweaty hour grooming him in the partial shade at the front of the barn after he'd gotten his oats. Besides, why rush home with Dad in such a foul mood and no friend to call on?

"It's just you and me, Whiskey," Lainey said. "You and me and maybe Ryan. But he'll go back to New York by the end of the summer." It gave her a pang to realize that Whiskey wasn't going to be around for long either. As soon as she got him trained enough so that other people could ride him, he'd be sold.

Mr. Dodge came out of his office. He hobbled toward them as if his joints were giving him trouble today. "Hear you had quite an adventure," he said. "Lopez says it was you brought Whiskey back."

"If Whiskey becomes reliable, couldn't you keep him on the ranch, Mr. Dodge?" she begged.

"Got to sell off some stock anyways," he said evasively. He eyed her under a wrinkled brow and confided, "Business isn't what it used to be, and me neither. I can't keep going like this. Got to sell Whiskey one way or another, Lainey. I'm sorry."

She groaned. If it didn't matter what she accomplished—if she was going to lose everybody she cared about, including Whiskey—what was the point of trying?

9

*M*om had been right about Dad. He had enough courage back by Monday to sit at the breakfast table reviewing old customers who might give him leads on remodeling jobs. Over his fried eggs and hash browns he even made Mom laugh about the customer who'd wanted a doghouse big enough for a bed so he could sleep there when his wife locked him out of their house.

"Lainey," Dad said, as he was about to leave, "I'm sorry if I talked mean to you on Saturday. You sure didn't deserve it."

"That's all right, Daddy."

He stood facing the door, as if he couldn't bring himself to face her, and his voice got husky as he added, "I just felt so bad about losing Cobb Lane and your having to move from here."

She caught her breath. They were moving? No one

had told her that. But she didn't say a word for fear her dismay might send him skidding back into despair.

She waited until he'd gone before asking her mother, "What did Dad mean, we have to move?"

Mom's plump shoulder rose in a shrug. "He thought I'd already gotten around to telling you, Lainey."

"Why *didn't* you tell me?"

"Because. You were dealing with so much bad news, I didn't see the sense in rushing to deliver the rest of it."

"We're losing everything?"

"Well, we're not quite out in the street yet, but the bank's taking over Cobb Lane Development at the end of the month. That's unless we can come up with enough of a payment on our loan to persuade them to extend it some more, and that's unlikely."

"The end of the month. That's less than two weeks," Lainey said.

"Don't look so tragic," Mom said. "Nobody's dying. We're just losing Cobb Lane and this house. That's the way it is with most builders when they start out. You put up a house, and if it doesn't sell, you move into it and wait for a buyer. Then you build another house and so on. Only this time we're not exactly selling. We took a risk and lost, that's all."

Lainey chewed on her lip, trying to absorb the bad news as her mother eyed her with concern. Finally, she said, "Mom, I'd appreciate it if you didn't keep things from me. I'm not a little girl you and Dad have to protect anymore. I'm part of this family, and I need to know what's going on in it."

Mom nodded. "Okay, from now on, I'll keep you posted. You'll get the news as it happens. I promise."

"So when're we moving?"

"Soon. I've started looking for a smaller place. We really don't need four bedrooms anyway with just the three of us."

Mom looked around her spacious kitchen, and even though her face didn't show regret, Lainey suspected it was there. Mom had handpicked the colorful Mexican tiles that made the kitchen so attractive. Most of her time at home was spent in this room cooking, or doing household bills at the built-in desk, or watching the portable TV from a counter stool.

"You really love this house, don't you, Mom?"

A lightning streak of pain flashed across Mom's face. "Yes, I love it, but a house is just a thing, Lainey, and things don't hurt too much to lose."

"They don't? They hurt me," Lainey said. She was thinking of the horse she didn't get for her birthday.

Mom gave her one of her cool blue looks. Quietly, she said, "I never had any ambitions like you and your brothers, Lainey. Your father was all I ever wanted. He's all I need."

Mom had not said her children were essential to her, Lainey noticed. But she wasn't surprised. She'd known that about Mom, that her husband came first with her. "You met Dad in high school, didn't you?" Lainey said now, to keep her mother talking.

"Yes, we were high school sweethearts." Mom set down the frying pan she had wiped clean. "I weighed too much even then, but he never cared. He *likes* big women." She flushed slightly and laughed and shook her head.

Having her mother talk intimately to her was so rare that Lainey wanted to hold on to the moment. "You *really* never thought about becoming anything like a nurse or a teacher?" she asked.

"No, I always figured who you loved mattered most. I never planned how I'd earn a living. I just knew I would somehow."

Thoughtfully, Lainey said, "It would be nice if you could find a house near here. I mean, so I could still walk to the ranch and over to Amber."

"I'll certainly try. . . . Lainey, there's no point worrying ahead of trouble. Just enjoy training your horse while you can." In a gesture unusual for her, Mom squeezed Lainey's shoulder.

Lainey took her mother's advice to heart. That week, she spent the whole of every day with Whiskey. Twice she got him past the quarter-mile mark, but both times he reversed direction and went back to the stable just when she thought she had him under control.

Chick razzed her about how much of Mr. Dodge's expensive feed she was wasting on Whiskey. Lopez said nothing, but he watched her all the time. When Mr. Dodge asked her if she'd had any luck with Whiskey yet, she was tempted to tell him about the times the horse had broken his quarter-mile limit. She held back only because she was afraid Whiskey would make a fool out of her if she boasted that he was obeying her— sometimes. Actually, he wasn't obeying, she suspected, just acting on his own whims.

It was Friday when Lainey led Whiskey up one of the state forest trails through saguaros high as telephone poles and onto a hilltop from which she could see the haze-coated sprawl of Tucson in the distance. That day it was she who decided when they should turn around, she who chose the paths they took through the rocky desert. Whiskey let her guide him with barely a touch of her leg on his side and a rein against his neck.

"So you're Mr. Good Boy today, huh, Whiskey?" she said. "Just the most amiable, best-behaved horse. How come? Are you in the mood to be good for a change, or is this the beginning of a new you?"

She loved the way his ears turned back to hear her when she spoke to him as if they were having a two-way conversation. And this time when she came riding with rocking chair ease back into the stables, she was ready to tell Mr. Dodge about Whiskey's progress.

They were all there as she dismounted. Mr. Dodge had come out of his office. Chick was holding a horse in front of the barn for Lopez, who was examining its hoof. And every eye was on her.

"You been gone all morning, Lainey," Mr. Dodge said. "Where'd you get to?"

"I don't know what it's called," she said, "but the hill where you can see Tucson? We went up that trail."

"You done it?" Chick chortled. "What'd you offer him, Lainey, a bushel of apples or an air-conditioned stall in the barn?"

"Whiskey just went where I told him," Lainey said. "Nothing to it."

Lopez curled his lips down as if he were impressed.

Mr. Dodge said, "Well, I'll be! I didn't really believe you could retrain an ornery, no-good, useless animal like this one, but you did it. Broke every rule in the book, and you did it." He shook his head in amazement. Then he added, "Well, you just keep breaking him in like you been doing, and if he stays broke, we'll sell him for a hefty price. He's looking like a quality horse now. Wouldn't you say, Lopez?"

"Top quality," Lopez said.

Lainey swung out of the saddle feeling as if she'd just won first prize for horsemanship. But in her heart she knew it wasn't what she had done, it was Whiskey. She planted a kiss on his spongy nose. When he rolled up his lips as if he were smiling, it made all the men laugh.

The daily trail rides continued without a hitch. Whiskey behaved as well as Lady or Shiloh. "My good buddy," Lainey called him often. "Look at what a sweetheart you can be." She didn't feel lonely when she was alone with him. His ears would turn to catch the sound of her voice as she mused aloud on what they were seeing or what she was thinking. He listened so intently that she became convinced he not only heard, but understood her.

Riding Whiskey made Lainey happy except when it struck her that she was training him for someone else's benefit. Then she cut to some other less painful thought. "Don't worry ahead of trouble," Mom had advised, and more and more Lainey was realizing how wise her mother was.

❧

On Thursday, Lainey was listening to Whiskey's hooves clopping musically against a rocky canyon floor when who should she see sitting on a boulder eating a picnic lunch but Amber.

"I can't believe you did it," Amber said.

"Did what?" Lainey asked in momentary confusion.

"Trained that horse good enough to ride him way up here."

"There wasn't much to training him. He's a great horse. He just needed some personal attention." Lainey smoothed his black mane over to one side of his neck.

"Are you going to get your dad to buy him for you?"

Lainey shook her head sorrowfully. "No chance." Then she asked, "*You* want to buy him, Amber?"

"Can't. I got Belle here, and my folks won't let me have more than one horse."

Lainey kept stroking Whiskey's neck, avoiding Amber's eyes, as she said, "I'd like a person who'll treat him right to buy him. He'd be best off as part of a family. He's got too much personality to be a hack anybody can rent."

"You're really stuck on that horse, aren't you?"

"I like him a lot, yeah," Lainey said.

"Too bad you can't keep him for yourself."

"Well, I can't." She kept her eyes on Whiskey's mane to hide the quick rise of tears the admission had brought.

"You know what you could do if you really want to get some private party interested in him?" Amber said. "You could show him off in the parade Saturday. That'd do it—if he shows good on parade."

"What parade?"

"The one to open the new park in Tucson where the old courthouse is. Didn't you hear about it? And they're holding a horse auction afterward. If Whiskey showed good and people spent big bucks for him, they'd treat him right. You know how it is; the most valuable horseflesh gets the best care."

That sounded reasonable. But Lainey said, "The only thing is Whiskey's not ready for a parade yet, Amber. He's still a little unpredictable, and I—"

"I'm going to be in it. You could ride with me. I'll even lend you my old riding outfit—that green one you admired? I got too big for it, but it should just fit you. Come on, Lainey, it'd be fun to do it together. Wouldn't it?"

"I thought you were mad at me."

"I was. When I saw you with that guy, I thought you were a traitor, dropping me for a boy just like any twitty girl would do. You know, it was bad enough when you couldn't see me because you had a job, but that *boy*—"

"He was never my boyfriend, Amber. He's just a kid from New York City that I was supposed to teach about horses."

As if she hadn't heard, Amber said, "You always say boys aren't interested in you, but they are. You just don't see it. Like in fourth grade, that kid who gave you the roses?"

"Oh, Amber! You still remember that? I was so embarrassed I wanted to die, and I wouldn't take the roses, and then the teacher came into the room. And that boy felt bad and I felt bad that he felt bad, and it was awful."

"Yeah, but he had a crush on you."

"So, big deal. He was a nerd and that was fourth grade."

"Okay, but I saw the way this guy from New York was looking at you, Lainey."

"How could you see anything? You loped by so fast you didn't even have time to wave."

"Have it your own way and don't believe me." Amber looked disgusted.

"Besides," Lainey said, "Ryan and I don't have anything in common. Like, he loves to read."

"Well, so do you."

Lainey hesitated. It was true that compared to someone like Amber who based her book reports on jacket flap copy alone, she, Lainey Cobb, was a reader. But she never thought of herself that way. What she read for mainly was information and to learn how to do something, while Ryan was a book person. He read for pleasure. And he wasn't really that interested in horses. He was a big-city boy. He didn't know cacti and lizards and snakes; he knew subways. It would take forever to explain all that to Amber, and she'd never believe it anyway. So let her think what she wanted. That way they wouldn't be likely to get mad at each other again.

"Amber, he's not my boyfriend," was all she said.

"You sure? . . . He was cute."

He *was* cute, Lainey thought, and she was sorry Ryan had disappeared from her life so fast, but he had. Briefly she wondered how his camping trip had come out. It certainly hadn't turned him into a horse lover because she hadn't seen him at Dodge's ranch for nearly two weeks. "Anyway," she said, "Ryan's only visiting in Tucson. So can we be friends again?"

"I guess," Amber said. "You're stubborn as a mule, but I miss you. Besides, you're the only friend I've got."

Lainey smiled into the flaxen-haired girl's fierce, square-jawed face. "I could say the same about you."

"So?"

"So, sure," Lainey said, "I'll ride in the parade with you. Or anyway, I'll give it a try."

She tethered Whiskey to the same tree Amber had used because it was the only vegetation around that didn't have prickers or spines on it. The two horses eyed each other, ears going back and forth as they snuffled in a non-threatening manner. Lainey watched them getting acquainted while Amber rattled on about Belle's recent horseshoeing experience. She'd kicked the farrier in punishment for his careless handling. "Belle's so smart. That klutz deserved to get kicked," Amber concluded, loyal to her horse as ever.

"Whiskey's smart, too," Lainey said.

"Yeah, well, then he should do okay in the parade."

Amber explained that anyone who wanted to enter it had to meet at the courthouse at 8:00 A.M. sharp Saturday. "The only thing is, to get from Dodge's ranch to the courthouse, you'll have to ride Whiskey over that metal bridge. You know, the one with the mesh bed? That could be a problem. Most horses balk because it clangs so loud when they step on it," Amber said.

"Well," Lainey said, "I've still got a few days. Maybe I can get him used to it." And to crowds of people, she was thinking, and to city traffic. And to who knew what else. It was asking a lot to expect Whiskey to get accustomed to all that in a few days. But then Whiskey might be capable of more than she imagined.

10

*T*hey separated at the main road. Amber went left to go home, and Lainey turned right toward Dodge's ranch. She wondered, as she entered it, if the ranch had seemed this dusty and run-down last summer. If it had, she hadn't noticed. Last summer she'd moved in a world that sparkled with promise. This summer it had dimmed considerably, and not just for her but for her parents and for Mr. Dodge.

What Mr. Dodge told her while she was unsaddling Whiskey dimmed Lainey's world even more. He gave her permission to ride Whiskey in the parade easily enough. It was what he said just before he hobbled off to answer the phone in his office that was the shocker.

She was standing there brooding about it as she picked the dirt out of Whiskey's hoof when a familiar voice interrupted her thoughts, "So how's the horse training going, Lainey?"

"Ryan! Hi. I haven't seen you around in a while." She smiled over her shoulder at him.

He leaned against the barn wall. "I've been recovering from the famous weekend camp-out with my father."

"Saddle sores?"

"Cactus spines in the butt."

She laughed briefly, then said, "I'm sorry."

"So was I. He brought me back slung over my horse belly down. Luckily I collided with the cactus on the way home, and we didn't have too far to ride."

"You fall or the horse pitch you off?" Lainey asked.

"More like the saddle slipped down to one side and I went with it. Dad claims I didn't tighten my cinch properly."

"Did he yell at you?"

"He's not the type to yell. He just looked so disgusted I wanted to slink into the nearest snake hole. I don't think he thinks I'm too bright."

"So it wasn't a good weekend."

"No, I wouldn't say that. My father talked a lot. I got closer to understanding him. In fact," Ryan said, "I suspect he's quite a guy. The problem is the feeling's not mutual."

"Just because you rolled off a horse?"

"No, just because I'm not the macho kid he'd like me to be."

"Oh." Lainey thought of her own father who also

preferred macho kids—male macho kids, not female substitutes.

"So, what's new with you and Whiskey?" Ryan asked.

"We're getting along great. We've been trail riding together every day."

"No kidding? That must make you happy."

"Sure, but—"

"But what?"

"Oh, Saturday there's a parade to open the new park in Tucson," Lainey said. "I'm going to try and ride Whiskey in that, and then if he does well, he'll get auctioned off to the highest bidder."

"That's no problem. Just don't do well and nobody will want him."

She moved to a rear hoof and, leaning into Whiskey, lifted his foot so that she could work on it. With her eyes focused on the hoof, Ryan wouldn't see her squeezing back the tears. It appalled her that tears threatened her so often lately.

"Mr. Dodge likes the parade idea," she said, and then she slipped Ryan the bad news Mr. Dodge had given her earlier. "Especially because he's selling off all his horses for whatever he can get for them. He says he's too old to run this operation anymore."

"You're kidding! The ranch is closing down?"

"Yup. Apparently Chick's already looking for another job. Lopez will stay on until the horses are gone. That's to help Mr. Dodge out. . . . Lady and Shiloh are going to a riding school that has mostly little kids. The best I can hope for Whiskey is that if he does well in the parade somebody nice will buy him."

"It doesn't seem fair when you worked so hard," Ryan said.

It wasn't fair, she thought, not because she'd worked hard on Whiskey but because she'd never love another horse as much. How could she when there'd never be one like him?

Ryan followed her as she led Whiskey to the corral and set him loose. Whiskey looked back at her as if to say, "So that's it for today?" Then he ambled over to check out the manger. Finding it empty, he shouldered his way into a group of horses standing in the mud by the water barrel and stuck his nose in the water to drink.

"So what are you here for?" Lainey asked Ryan.

"Oh, I thought I'd visit with Chester and see if he feels like hauling me around on his back for a while. My father's got some business down at the hotel, so he dropped me off for an hour or so."

"Today I'm going to walk Whiskey through some heavy traffic and maybe around a shopping plaza. That'll take a lot longer than an hour," Lainey said. "But tomorrow I've got to try him on a bridge he'll have to cross to get to the start of the parade. Want to ride with me then?" She hoped Ryan wouldn't think she was flirting; she just wanted a chance to see him again.

"Sure. Why not?"

"I mean, Whiskey likes riding with other horses," she

added hastily to put a different cast on her invitation. "And if you rode Chester—"

"It might keep Whiskey calmer. Sure." Ryan sounded pleased.

Lainey wondered if he liked her. She was only just discovering how much she liked him.

⁂

Dad came home with two small bunches of store-bought flowers—red carnations for Mom, and pink and white ones for Lainey. "For my two best girls," Dad said.

"What're we celebrating?" Mom asked after admiring the flowers and thanking him.

"Remember the old man who gave me such a hard time about the addition to his house?"

"The high-voiced one with the fancy silver buckle?"

"Right. He wants me to build a house for him and his new wife." Dad grinned. "Seems he got himself married to a lady half his age, and she doesn't like his old place."

"Well, good for him and good for us."

"Then we don't have to move?" Lainey asked.

Dad's face fell. "It's not that good, Lainey. We're still losing Cobb Lane—all of it. This job'll just pay our other bills for a while."

"I found us a house," Mom said.

"Where?" Lainey asked.

"A mile or so back of where your friend Amber lives.

It'll be a long way from the ranch, but don't worry. I'll drive you."

"You won't have to. Mr. Dodge is going out of business anyway."

"Is that so? Well, too bad, but I'm not surprised," Dad said. "Losing his wife took the heart out of him."

"Or he just decided he's old enough to retire," Mom said. "After all, a ranch like that is a lot of work."

Her parents' eyes focused on Lainey. Afraid their sympathy would bring on the sudden tears again, she changed the subject by saying, "So you found a house? A little one?"

"It's smaller than this," Mom said, "and a few years older, but I think you'll both like it. It's got a nice wide porch across the front and plenty of space out back."

Dad stretched his long arms up so that he almost touched the ceiling. "That doesn't sound too bad."

"When are we moving?" Lainey asked.

"I told them by the end of next week." Mom watched her as if she feared Lainey might erupt at the news.

"I'm thirsty," Lainey murmured and went for a glass of ice water. She hoped they wouldn't be able to see from her back any sign of the hard lump stuck in her chest.

That night she couldn't seem to fall asleep. She was remembering how excited they'd all been the day they'd moved into Cobb Lane. Everything in the brand-new house, the first that Dad had built as his own boss, gleamed and smelled new. Lainey had gloated over her bedroom being big enough to have an extra bed in it for a friend to sleep over. She had reveled in her walk-in closet and enjoyed stowing her belongings in it. Mom had admired the golden oak cabinets and her fancy kitchen tiles. Dad had even talked about there being space out back for a pool someday.

Well, they'd had two good years here. And as Mom would point out, nobody was sick or dying. Dad's business could always turn and go up instead of down. They might even build another house here or buy back this one. But more than the house, she'd miss Dodge's ranch. And more than the ranch, she would miss Whiskey.

He had to behave himself well at that parade. If he didn't, and Mr. Dodge was left to sell him, it would go bad for Whiskey. She wondered if the horse would understand if she tried to explain it to him. He had to understand. "None of your tricks now," she'd tell him. "This is serious business. In fact, your life depends on it."

11

*R*yan was getting out of his father's Range Rover when Lainey arrived at the ranch Thursday morning. From what she could see of Ryan's father through the car window, he wouldn't win any macho-male contest himself, so why should he be disappointed in his son? A thick layer of soft flesh hid the shape of the man's bones. Only his wiry gray hair showed vigor.

"Looks like they had a big trail ride this morning. The corral's pretty empty," Ryan said to Lainey after his father took off. "I hope Chester's still around."

"How come that goofy horse is your favorite, Ryan?"

Ryan's grin brought dimples to his cheeks. "Chester and I are simpatico."

She grinned back at him. "You mean you like to chew on things?"

"I mean, we've both got oddball habits. He chews and I read. Why do you like Whiskey?"

She thought about it. "Whiskey's a great horse. He's beautiful and smart and—"

"Hard to manage," Ryan put in.

She ignored that. "And he's playful, and I like that he's got a mind of his own."

"An independent horse for an independent girl."

She wrinkled her nose. "Sort of."

"So today we see if he'll go over that bridge for you, huh?"

"Right. It's the last thing I need to test him on before the parade. He did fine in traffic yesterday." She saw Whiskey watching her from inside the corral and went to the fence to give him the bread she'd brought. He took it neatly, then nuzzled her shoulder.

"Is he saying thank you, or asking for more?" Ryan asked.

"He's saying, 'Hi, glad to see you,' " she said.

"Amazing," Ryan teased. "Only two legs and you can understand horse language."

"Whiskey's my best buddy." She kissed his spongy nose, and Whiskey lifted his lip in that horsey smile of his.

Ryan laughed. "I didn't know a horse could do that," he said.

Lainey didn't respond. She was thinking that she and Whiskey had only today, tomorrow, and the parade, and then if someone bought him, he'd be gone from her life forever. The thought depressed her.

Chester was busy rubbing his head against a loose

fence railing. "There's my horse," Ryan said. "They should have called him Termite, the way he's drawn to wood. How about I get a head start on saddling him while you tell Dodge we're here?"

Lainey nodded and walked over to the office, leaving Whiskey at the railing.

Mr. Dodge looked up from the morning news on his TV. His eyes were red rimmed as if he'd been crying. "What's wrong?" she asked him.

"They're gone, Lainey. Lopez is leading Lady and Shiloh over to the kids' camp. And last night they came down with a horse van from that hotel up in red country and took off the best of what I had left." His voice cracked, and he took out a handkerchief and blew his nose.

"Oh, Mr. Dodge, I'm sorry. But why did you sell the horses if it makes you feel so bad?"

"Had to. The only sensible thing for an old party like me. I got to provide for myself, you know. Can't just—" He sighed. "Besides, them horses'll be better off up north in Sedona. The summers are cooler, and there's grass maybe." He sniffed. "Don't mind me. I got nothing to be weepy about. Just getting soft in the head."

She gave him a clean tissue from her pocket and walked around the desk to pat his shoulder while he blew his nose again. "You didn't sell Whiskey, though," she said. "Did the people from the hotel want him?"

"Well, they asked about him. But you and me got a deal going on that horse," Mr. Dodge said. "I couldn't sell him out from under you before the parade, not after the job you did training that animal. I'm looking to be proud of you on Saturday."

"You're not going to watch, are you?" she asked in alarm.

"Sure I am," Mr. Dodge said. "Wouldn't miss it for the world."

"Oh, boy!" Lainey said. "I wasn't thinking about having an audience."

Now it was Mr. Dodge's turn to pat her shoulder. "You'll do fine," he assured her.

Of course, she realized, she had to do fine and so did Whiskey because if no one bid on him at the auction—if he didn't show well—he could still end up being sold by the pound to be made into dog meat.

"Chick called last night," Mr. Dodge said. "He got himself a bartending job. Said he's sick of smelling like a horse and not earning enough to buy himself a new car. Can't blame him, young fellow like him."

"Lopez won't stop being a wrangler, will he?" Lainey asked.

"Him? No. He likes horses a whole lot better than people. Got himself a wife about the same time he got Chico. He didn't handle the wife too good and lost her, but he turned Chico into a first-rate working horse. So long as there's horses to handle, Lopez won't have no trouble finding himself a job." Mr. Dodge fixed his gaze on Lainey. "You know, I would've hired you like I promised if I'd've stayed in business. Can't get over what you done with Whiskey."

"I still have to try him out on that metal bridge."

Mr. Dodge grunted. "Oh, yeah. The one over the irrigation canal. Forgot you have to get him to cross that. . . . Listen, if he don't want to go across, don't you try and force him, hear? I don't want nothing happening to you."

Ryan was already mounted on Chester and waiting for Lainey at the corral gate when she brought the tack out of the barn for Whiskey.

"I'm going to miss this place," Ryan said as she let herself into the corral. "It's been fun riding here."

"There are other ranches in town. Your father will probably drop you off at another one just as easy," she said.

"Maybe he could pick you up and you could come with me?"

The invitation pleased her, but Lainey said, "I may be gone, too, Ryan." Briefly she told him about her family's moving plans.

"You won't leave without giving me your address, will you? I mean, you're the only other kid I know in this town. You don't want me knocking on doors all over Tucson asking if they can tell me where Lainey is."

She laughed. "You know what they'd say? They'd say, 'Who's Lainey?' "

"Wanna bet? That parade's going to make you famous."

"You mean when Whiskey goes wild and runs up the courthouse steps?"

"Come on," he said. "You've got that horse eating out of your hand. He wouldn't go wild with you on his back."

She didn't think he would. But as she saddled Whiskey, she couldn't help worrying. When his hooves clanged on that metal bridge and nothing felt normal to him, would he go crazy? He might.

Before mounting Whiskey, Lainey checked the cinch Ryan had buckled on Chester and adjusted the lengths of Ryan's stirrups.

"You know, Lainey," he said, "if you were a guy, you'd be just the kind of kid my father would like."

"If I were a guy? But I'm not." Lainey spoke more sharply than she intended.

"Hey," he said. "I didn't mean that the way it came out. I mean, it's great you're a girl. It's—"

"Come on, Ryan," she interrupted his embarrassed sputtering. "Let's go. I want to be on that bridge before the sun gets too hot."

She swung into the saddle and led the way along the verge of the road. They walked the two horses the whole three miles. Passing Cobb Lane, Lainey held her breath as usual, but Whiskey kept moving as if he'd forgotten this was the spot where he used to about-face. His lean cheeks swayed just ahead of her hands as he clopped along, ignoring the cars and trucks passing a few feet away. The slow motion would have put Lainey to sleep if she hadn't been so keyed up.

"Now, Whiskey, this bridge we're going to cross may feel strange to you," she warned him. "But it's just a little bridge, not that wide and not that long, and if you keep to the deck part, you won't have to step on the mesh at all. And even if you do step on the mesh part, your feet are too big to get caught in those little holes. Really, you don't have to worry about a thing."

"Sounds as if you're the one who's worried," Ryan said.

"Maybe a little, but he's going to do it. He'll just cross that bridge as if he's been doing it all his life. Won't you, Whiskey? Won't you?" She patted him and talked nonsense to him. Meanwhile, his ears flicked back to listen as if the sound of her voice were entertaining him on the long, hot, dull walk.

A rabbit started up behind a yucca. Whiskey ignored it.

They stopped for a red light. When it changed, Whiskey again started easily at Lainey's signal.

"There it is," she said, pointing. "You can see it."

"That little span?" Ryan asked. "That's what you're worried about?"

"Um-hmm." Her throat was too dry to keep talking. Still she made herself chatter on to Whiskey.

"I wonder how you got your name, anyway? I bet some fool cowboy named you. But you're too dark a brown to be the color of liquor, except when I brush you up real good. Then you gleam red in the sun, don't you?" She brushed a fly off his neck. "Tomorrow for the parade, I'll come early and curry you and brush you and rub your hair and comb your mane until you shine.

Tonight I'll even oil the saddle we're going to use, and I'll brush my hair until it shines, too. And—"

Whiskey's hooves touched the metal mesh and rang out tinnily as she had expected, but his stride didn't change. He walked calmly onto the deck that was laid like a hall runner over the roadway. Though his hoof-beats made a hollow noise on the deck, it didn't seem to bother him.

Midway across the bridge Whiskey stopped. Lainey's heart gave a jolt and stopped, too. He leaned his head over the railing and looked down.

"Oh-oh," Ryan said.

Lainey clucked at Whiskey and said, "Come on, now, there's nothing interesting down there, and it's much too far to jump." As if he agreed, he continued walking, with Chester following placidly.

And then they were back on a normal roadway.

"Let's turn around and do it over again," she said.

"It sure doesn't look as if you're going to have any problem with him," Ryan said. "You've really got that horse trained, Lainey."

"I hope so," she said.

It thrilled her when Whiskey returned the way he'd come without even bothering to peer over the railing this time.

Halfway back to the ranch, Lainey was rocking peacefully in the saddle, thinking that she would iron her white cotton shirt and tie a red bandanna around her neck to go with the green riding pants Amber had lent her for the parade. She was dazed with the heat and half asleep when, without warning, a carload of teenage boys whizzed by, blowing a horn that sounded like a bellowing bull. The boys hiked up in their seats and turned to see if the blast had made the horses bolt.

At the sound, Whiskey had jerked his head and danced sideways, but he settled quickly to Lainey's pull of the reins and her voice saying, "It's okay, Whiskey. Nothing bad's happening. It's okay, boy."

It was Chester who reacted violently. He gave a high-pitched whinny and dashed off the road across a bare field studded with creosote bush and cholla. Ryan was in danger of losing his seat. His arms were flapping like wings, and his reins hung loose. Lainey gave chase. It didn't take long for Whiskey to pull abreast of Chester.

"Tighten up your reins and pull back on them," Lainey told Ryan. Whiskey ran in step with Chester, slowing as Lainey sat back in the saddle and drew back on her reins. Chester slowed too, first to a trot and finally to a walk. He was foaming at the mouth and dripping sweat. Terror showed in the whites of his eyes.

"Wow, that was some ride!" Ryan said. "If you hadn't rescued me, we'd be in the next county. Thanks."

"That's okay. You stayed on fine, Ryan. I guess you can sit a horse now. Maybe you ought to ride in the parade with me."

"Me? No way. I only stayed on to avoid another butt full of cactus spines."

She laughed. Ryan put himself down a lot, but he

was capable of more than just reading books, she'd noticed. They turned the horses and trotted them back toward the road.

"What now?" Ryan asked in alarm as Chester halted for no reason in the middle of the field.

"He's urinating. You should stand up in the stirrups to relieve the pressure on his kidneys."

Ryan groaned and said, "He runs away with me, and you want me to worry about his kidneys? Give me a break, Lainey." But he stood up as she'd suggested. "You know, I'd like to come and watch you in that parade," he said. "Unless my father has other plans. He did say something about a surprise for me on Saturday."

"It'd be nice to have my own cheering section," Lainey said, delighted at the hope of seeing Ryan again.

"Oh, there'll be plenty of people cheering you," he said. "Your parents will come, won't they?"

"Not both of them. Saturdays are a busy day for them. But Mr. Dodge may be there. Anyway, I hope Whiskey behaves as well as he did on this ride." She patted Whiskey's shoulder and asked with pride, "Wasn't he a trouper on the bridge, and when those kids tried to spook us?"

They were close to Cobb Lane when Whiskey suddenly neighed and began rearing.

Out of the corner of her eye, as she fought to master Whiskey, Lainey saw her father's truck. He was coming home early. "Oh, no," she said out loud. What a disaster to have Dad see Whiskey going loco! Lainey was gripping hard with her knees and trying to calm Whiskey down with her voice while she hung onto the saddle horn and managed the reins. She was too busy to worry about being thrown.

Ryan rode Chester out of her way onto the verge of the road and stopped. Dad pulled the truck off the road and leaped out to run to her.

Desperately, Lainey begged, "Down, boy. Easy, Whiskey. Whoa, whoa."

The sound of her voice had no effect on him, nor did her attempt to rein him in. He plunged into the roadway and began bucking. Then she saw it! A bee was biting Whiskey's haunch and driving him crazy. She reached back and smacked the bee hard with her bare hand. She'd hit it; she could feel the lump of its body before it fell to the ground.

"Lainey!" Dad was reaching for the reins, standing close to Whiskey's head. "Are you all right?"

"I'm fine," she said. Just then Whiskey reared up, neighing in panic as Dad laid a hand on him. The next instant Lainey lost a stirrup and fell off, hitting her shoulder on the roadway.

"Lainey!" her father shouted. Ryan cried out something, but what she heard was Whiskey's frenzied hoofbeats retreating in the distance as he galloped back to the ranch.

Her father lifted her off the road and out of the path of the oncoming traffic.

"She shouldn't be moved if she broke anything," Ryan said.

"You want her to get hit by a car instead?" Dad growled.

"I'm okay. I just slipped off. I didn't break anything," Lainey assured him. She pushed her father away from her and stood up to prove it. Her shoulder ached fiercely and so did her hip, but she said, "Really, I'm fine. It was just—"

"That's it," her father interrupted her tersely. "You will not ride that horse again—ever—for any reason."

"But Dad, it wasn't his fault."

"Not much it wasn't."

"He got stung by a *bee*," Lainey shrieked to make him understand.

"I don't care. He could have killed you."

"Dad!"

"No," he said. "I don't want to hear another word. Come into the house, Lainey. I want your mother to look you over." He marched off without waiting to see if she'd follow his order and without any farewell niceties to Ryan.

"Oh, boy," Ryan murmured. "I guess Whiskey's not going to be in that parade after all."

"Yes he is," Lainey said with icy certainty. "When Dad calms down, he'll realize it was the bee's fault. Whiskey's okay. Everybody jumps around when a bee stings them."

Ryan was grinning. "You and that horse are some pair, Lainey." He shook his head and remounted Chester, who was chewing on the thin branch of a paloverde tree in front of the Cobb Lane arch. "Well, I'll go see if Whiskey made it back to the ranch. Good luck with your father." He saluted her and rode off.

She should have given him her address, Lainey thought, but she had more important things to think about. Like convincing her father that he *had* to let her ride Whiskey in the parade.

12

"*M*om," Lainey cried as she ran into the kitchen, "where did he go?"

"Who?" The potato in Mom's hand halted in mid-peel.

"Dad. He saw my horse acting up, so he came rushing over and scared Whiskey so I fell off, and then—" Lainey gulped for air. "And *then* he said I couldn't ride in the parade, which is just—"

"I'm here," Dad said. He stepped into the room, somber as a thundercloud, obviously having overheard every word.

"Dad, you can't mean it about the parade. Whiskey got stung by a *bee. Anybody* jumps around when a bee's stinging them. And then you scared him because he doesn't know you."

"Any horse that startles that easily isn't fit to ride in a parade." Dad folded his arms across his chest. His lips set in a grim negative.

"Mom!" Lainey turned to her mother, who was getting on with her potato peeling.

"Calm down, Lainey. Arguing in the state you're in won't win you anything." Mom's eyes were sending a warning that Lainey was too keyed up to heed.

"But what Dad saw was just a—just a fluke," Lainey insisted. "Whiskey's been so *good* in traffic. He didn't even jump when a car full of kids blasted their horn in his ear today. And he walked over the bridge that I was sure would spook him without acting nervous at all. He's as safe to ride as any horse in the *world*. It's just that he got stung by a—"

"Bee, I know. I heard you, Lainey," Mom said. She looked at Dad, who seemed to have turned to stone, and back at Lainey. Very quietly, Mom said, "We'll discuss it after dinner, okay?"

"No," Lainey said. "I'm just upset because Dad's being unfair, and I want to talk about it right now."

"You say any more and you'll make matters worse," Mom warned. She kept peeling away as if that homely chore would immunize her from the emotion charging around her. "As things stand *right now*, your father saw the incident and he thinks your horse isn't safe to ride."

"Because he saw me fall. But so what if I fell off? Riders fall off horses all the time, and nobody stops riding because of it."

"That horse could kill you, Lainey," Dad said.

"Whiskey loves me. And I love him. And I *have* to

ride him in the parade Saturday. I have to or he'll be sold for dog meat." She glared at her father with clenched fists.

"I can't let you risk your neck just because you'll be mad at me if I don't let you," Dad said in a sorrowful voice. "What kind of a parent would I be if I gave in to that kind of blackmail?"

"But Dad, why *can't* you let me risk my neck? You let Lon and Pete risk theirs. If I were a boy, you'd let me ride in that parade, wouldn't you?"

He hesitated. "Seems to me we've had this discussion before, Lainey. You're not a boy."

"But I can ride as well as any boy. Ask Mr. Dodge, ask Lopez. Lopez knows more about horses than anybody. He's Mr. Dodge's right-hand man, and *he* thinks I'm doing great with Whiskey."

"Let Lopez ride him in the parade, then," Dad said.

"But I trained Whiskey, and I'm the one he'll show his best for. Please, Dad. It was just a bee." She hated the tears filming her eyes, but she couldn't hide them because she needed to latch eyes with her father.

He looked at his wife. "Tell her, Connie," he said.

"Tell her what?"

"That I'm right."

"I'm not sure you are, Randall."

"Why can't you ever back me up in these things?" he snapped.

Mom stopped peeling to stare at him.

"You better look your daughter over to make sure

she didn't break any bones," he added before he stomped out of the room.

"I don't know, Lainey," Mom said. "They *told* me girls were a lot harder to raise than boys. Now I'm beginning to believe them." She set the potatoes aside, washed and dried her hands, and said, "Come in the bathroom and let's see what you did to yourself."

Lainey's shoulder was bruised and scraped under her shirt. Mom put antiseptic on it and said it would be sore for a while but nothing seemed broken. "We better get some ice on that shoulder, and on the hip, too," Mom said when she saw the bigger bruise spreading on Lainey's hip. "You aren't going to feel much like riding in that parade Saturday."

"You'd let me go, wouldn't you, Mom?"

Mom thought about it before nodding. "Probably," she said. "You know, as a kid I resented being told I couldn't do something as well as a boy. But I never was one to fight the system, and I'm happy being the kind of woman my parents expected me to be. You, though, I can see you've got more of your father in you than you have of me—more than your brothers have in some ways." Mom ran a knuckle tenderly down Lainey's cheek. "But battling your father head-on is no way to win," she admonished. "Try being patient, Lainey."

"I don't have time to be patient. The parade is Saturday."

Mom stood up. "All right," she said. "I know that horse means a lot to you. I'll see what I can do with your father . . . *after* we give him some time to get over his scare. Meanwhile, go lie down and I'll bring you some ice packs."

Dinner was eaten in a brooding silence. In silence, Dad helped Mom with the dishes. In silence, he left to watch his news program. He sat in his favorite chair across from the TV. Lainey settled on the couch with the ice bag on her hip and ice wrapped in a kitchen towel on her shoulder. She did ache, but she knew that no matter how bruised and sore she felt, it couldn't stop her from riding Whiskey—not when his fate was in her hands.

Friday morning at breakfast Dad looked up from his eggs ranchero and said, "I haven't changed my mind, Lainey, but your mother thinks I ought to see what Dodge says about that horse. If you want, I'll take you over to the ranch before I leave for work."

"Thanks, Dad," Lainey said. A good night's sleep had cooled her temper and sweetened her tongue. She smiled at her mother, who winked at her over her coffee cup.

"That was the best I could do for you," Mom said later when they were alone in the kitchen. "I hope it works out the way you want, Lainey."

Lainey kissed her mother and hugged her hard. "Did I ever tell you what a great mother you are?" Mom flushed with pleasure, as if she wasn't used to receiving compliments from Lainey.

Come to think of it, Lainey told herself, it was always

Dad who got the compliments and kisses, and Dad to whom she attached herself whenever they went anyplace as a family. Mom had to make do with the printed message in birthday or Mother's Day cards. That would have to be changed from now on, Lainey decided.

In the truck she began selling her father on Whiskey's good points. "See, Whiskey's smarter than most horses, Dad. So he makes up his own mind about things, which is why you can't always predict what he's going to do."

"You mean he's not reliable," Dad said.

"I didn't say that. He likes me, so he does what I ask him to do. Except—"

"Except if he doesn't feel like it."

"Dad, really! Let me introduce you to him before you decide he's no good. He's spirited, that's all."

Dad pulled the truck up to the ramada. One of the tree trunks that held up the roof had cracked, and the corner of the roof was sagging. "Dodge sure is letting the place run down," Dad muttered.

As usual, Mr. Dodge was sitting in his office desk chair in front of the TV. He gave a big smile when Lainey and her father walked in. "Well, look who's here! Haven't seen you in a long time, Randall Cobb. How's it going?"

"Fine, fine. Business could be better, though. How about you, Dodge?"

"Well, I'm about done with the ranch, Randall. Best thing I got left around here is your daughter. She's some girl. The way she's brought that useless horse around—you know about how she's trained Whiskey, don't you?"

"Whiskey is what I came to talk to you about." Dad took the seat Mr. Dodge offered. He didn't look very comfortable balancing his large body on the narrow wooden chair, with his long legs bent up like a stepladder.

Getting right down to business, Dad asked, "Would you say that horse is safe for Lainey to ride in the parade?"

"Safe?" Mr. Dodge's eyebrows went up to his hairline, stacking up ridges in his forehead. "Well, now, as to safe, I don't know what is. Crossing the road, you're as like to be killed by a car as not. And horses—well, there's always something you haven't figured on."

"Whiskey threw her yesterday. I happened to be coming home, and I saw him behaving like a bucking bronco."

"A bee stung him, Mr. Dodge," Lainey put in.

"There, yes, that's what I mean," Mr. Dodge said. "Something you haven't figured on, like a bee sting. That'll spook an animal so it throws you. . . . You get hurt, Lainey?"

"No, I'm fine. Dad doesn't want me to ride Whiskey tomorrow, Mr. Dodge. Please tell him it's okay."

"Well now, I can't promise it will be, Lainey." He turned to her father. "You know, Randall, I wouldn't have let her work with the horse if it was a mean one or if it—but there's no guarantee that something couldn't happen. Especially with all the goings-on in a parade."

"But Whiskey's a good horse now, isn't he?" Lainey pursued urgently. "I mean riding any horse in the parade would be the same risk, right?"

"Well . . ." Mr. Dodge sat there nodding to himself in an anxious silence. Finally he bent forward and said earnestly to Lainey's father, "I just can't give you any guarantee, you see?"

"I see," Dad said.

Lainey stood up. "Dad," she pleaded. "Come out to the corral and meet Whiskey. Let me show you how he listens to me."

"I don't have all day to spend on this, and meeting the horse isn't going to change my mind any," Dad said.

"Just come with me." She dragged him out of the office and over to the corral fence by one arm.

Whiskey was frisking around the open shed. Trotting in and out of the sorry-looking leftovers from the sale to the hotel in Sedona, he appeared to be doing some kind of square dance all by himself. Even if he hadn't been moving, he would have stood out among those old, swaybacked, knobby-legged horses.

"Look at him, Daddy. Isn't he beautiful?"

"He's a nice-looking animal. Yes, I'll grant you that."

Lainey whistled her two-note call, and Whiskey pricked up his ears and faced her across the corral. Even stock-still, he vibrated with energy.

She left her father outside the fence and entered the corral. "Whiskey," she called.

Abruptly, he broke into a gallop and came racing full out, straight for her. The double-time pounding of his hoofbeats started up a pounding echo in Lainey's chest. What had gotten into Whiskey? Was he planning to run her down? And, with Dad watching, why did Whiskey have to start acting crazy when she wanted Dad to see how well behaved he was!

"Lainey, get out of his way. Move it," Dad yelled. He was wrestling the corral gate open, but it seemed to be stuck.

She stood with her legs braced, perfectly still as Whiskey flew at her, nostrils flaring, like some wild stallion on the attack. Fear struck an ax blade through her chest. She had to jump. But which way? Suddenly there he was, looming over her, huge and powerful.

And then Whiskey stopped short.

He was so close, his yeasty breath tickled her cheek. Mischievously, he bumped her shoulder with his warm nose as if to say, "Scared you, didn't I?"

"That crazy animal could've killed you," Dad shouted. "Why didn't you move, Lainey?"

"Because I knew he wouldn't hurt me," she said.

Lopez had come up on Chico without their being aware of him. Dad noticed him now and turned toward him.

"This is my father, Lopez," Lainey said. "He thinks Whiskey's a dangerous animal."

Lopez's lips lifted in a disdainful smile. His beard had come in well, and he looked more like a dapper, modern-day conquistador than ever.

"You don't think this horse is safe for a little girl like her, do you?" Dad asked.

"She can handle him," Lopez said.

"Please, Dad," Lainey begged. "Whiskey was just teasing. He didn't mean any harm."

"He could cripple you not meaning any harm."

"But I've told you, Dad—I *have* to ride him in the parade."

Whiskey bumped Lainey's sore shoulder gently with his nose again. She winced but didn't budge.

"You're supposed to be expert with horses," Dad said to Lopez in a strained voice.

Lopez looked him straight in the eye without responding.

"Just tell me this. If she were your daughter, would you let her ride this horse tomorrow?"

"If she were mine, I'd trust her," Lopez said in a quiet voice. "I'd be proud of her, and I'd trust her." He waited half a minute while Dad stood there looking stunned, then he clip-clopped off into the corral on Chico.

Dad eyed Lainey through the heavy silence between them.

She faced him, nearly bursting with the confidence Lopez's approval had given her, but all she said was, "He'd trust me, Dad. Can't you?"

He rubbed his chin with his big hand and groaned. "I've taken a lot of risks in my life and come out a loser, Lainey. If I risk you—"

"You won't lose, Daddy. I promise you. Whiskey and I are going to do fine in that parade. You'll see."

"All right. All right. I do trust you. I do. You can ride him, but for my sake, Lainey, you just better be careful." He put his arms around her and held her close, as if he'd like to keep her safe there forever.

Meanwhile, Whiskey pawed the ground, softly blowing out air and waiting for Lainey.

13

"**Y**ou've got to be at the courthouse at eight sharp," Amber said over the phone.

Lainey looked at the clock. It was only 5:00 A.M. "You should have called me earlier, Amber," Lainey teased. "How am I ever going to make it in three hours?"

"I only just woke up," Amber protested. Anxiously, she asked, "You need any help?"

"Just kidding. I got everything ready last night. All I have to do is get Whiskey and trot on over. I'll be there. Don't worry." She smiled into the receiver as Amber breathed out a whoosh of relief and hung up.

It was cool in the dim light of dawn. Lainey listened, but it seemed the ringing of the phone hadn't awakened her parents. The house still rested quietly in the lap of sleep. Amber's riding pants, the blouse Lainey had ironed last night, and the boots she'd polished were packed in a gym bag. All she had to do was slip on her old jeans and sneakers, eat a peanut butter sandwich, and leave. Her parents knew she'd be leaving early, but she wrote a note saying she was off. Then she started walking to the ranch.

Today might be the last time she took this road, she thought. Another week and they'd be moving. She'd have to come by to see Mr. Dodge, of course, although visiting the ranch once Whiskey was gone would be depressing. She didn't want to even imagine how much she'd miss him. But no matter, Whiskey had to find a new owner. He had to look so fine in this parade today that some rich girl would buy him and give him his own paddock and plenty of good feed and lots of loving attention.

Lainey's lip trembled. It wasn't fair. It wasn't fair that she couldn't keep Whiskey herself. It wasn't fair that Dad's business was failing. He worked so hard, and he was such a good man. Well, and she was a good girl and Whiskey was a good horse, and Mr. Dodge was good, too, and look what was happening to him! "Life isn't always fair," Mom would say. And then she'd smile and add that no matter, you just had to keep chugging along doing your best. Shape up and stop sniveling, Lainey told herself. The rider had to look good, too, on parade.

Whiskey was one of the few horses in the corral who seemed to be awake. Lainey could smell the warm, rank horseflesh in the dewy air of early morning. It was an odor she loved, and she couldn't imagine why her father objected to the smell on her.

"Come on, Whiskey. We have to make you beautiful. Today's your big day," she told him when her whistle brought him to her.

He snuffled, and she kissed his doughy muzzle. "Have I ever told you I love you, Whiskey?" she whispered, as if anyone were around to hear her. Saying it made her eyes fill up again. Impatiently, she shook her head. No time for tears this morning.

She'd forgotten to bring a halter from the barn, but she only needed her arm on Whiskey's neck to make him follow her through the corral gate and over to the hitching rail. There she had a moment of anxiety. If she let go of him and he ran away now, it was her own stupid fault for not thinking ahead. "Whiskey, you stay here a second, okay? I'll bring you some oats," she bribed. Then she rushed into the barn and grabbed the nearest halter. Whiskey was right behind her when she turned. He'd followed her into the barn.

She chuckled and said, "Oh, you. When are you going to listen to what I tell you and just do it, huh?" She laid her cheek against his and led him back outside to the rail.

He munched contentedly on the bucket of oats she'd promised him while she gave him his last brushing. "You're going to be the best-looking horse in that parade today," she assured him.

The sun was roof high when she finished. Its rays struck reddish embers from Whiskey's mink brown hair. Lainey gave her favorite saddle a last rubdown. She'd already cleaned and oiled it. It took her less than a minute to change into her riding pants and shirt and leave her work clothes in the gym bag in the barn. Finally, she fitted the bridle over Whiskey's narrow head. "You know how special today is, don't you?" she asked him. His eyes studied her. Of course he did. He understood everything. Nobody would ever convince her he didn't.

"The best horse in the parade," she crooned to him. "Just the very best."

"Came out to wish you luck," Mr. Dodge said. He was walking with a cane today, Lainey saw. Like the ranch, he seemed to be deteriorating fast.

"How are you, Mr. Dodge?"

"Not bad. Not bad. You got Whiskey shined up like a show horse. We should get a fortune for him at the auction."

"What I want to get is a good home for him."

"Well, whatever happens, you done a good job. How'd you make your dad change his mind about letting you ride? He sure didn't sound like he was going to give in yesterday."

"It was Lopez," she said. "Something Lopez said." She lifted herself lightly into the saddle.

"That so? Well, Lopez must think pretty highly of you, Lainey. He don't have much good to say about two-legged creatures as a rule, especially not female ones." Mr. Dodge patted Whiskey's rump. "You both look like winners. Think he'll go over that bridge okay?"

"He didn't have any problem with it yesterday."

"Is that so? Well, good luck, then. I'll see you at the

park. I hear the auction'll be held by the new ball field parking lot. Should be easy to find."

"Should be. I'll see you, Mr. Dodge."

She adjusted her battered felt hat. It was the only thing she was wearing besides her boots that didn't look crisp and new. "This'll be your lucky hat," Dad had told her when he gave it to her—back in the days when Cobb Builders promised to be a big success and there was sure to be a horse to go with the hat eventually. Never mind, she told herself; this morning she was riding the horse she would choose if she could have any in the world.

Whiskey rocked her along steadily in the saddle on the long trek to the courthouse. She even let him trot for a while when they were still on the outskirts of town, where traffic was light and there was plenty of undeveloped land alongside the road. Today Whiskey's trot was so smooth she barely bounced in the saddle with it, and trotting ate up the ground faster. They'd get to the courthouse early, but that would be a plus. It would allow Whiskey time to get used to the crowd and the other horses in the parade.

There it was, the bridge over the irrigation ditch. She could just see its metal arch gleaming dully in the distance.

But what was happening on it? An accident? Two police cars with top lights flashing blocked the middle of the bridge. Men were setting up barricades. And a couple of cars were sprawled at awkward angles. It looked as if they were still allowing a single lane of traffic across the bridge, though.

Lainey slowed Whiskey to a walk and approached the bottleneck cautiously. If he had to cross the bridge on the mesh rather than on the deck, she didn't want to try it when any cars were also crossing. She held Whiskey back until a car passed and then a truck. He began to toss his head and dance his feet about impatiently. When she set him walking toward the bridge again, she told him, "Relax, Whiskey, it's just a little narrower today, that's all. You can do it. No problem for a steady guy like you." But she could feel the pulling of his neck.

A sudden rise of his body and Whiskey bolted.

He flew straight for the three-foot barricade and leaped it as if it weren't there. His feet touched the deck. Then he careened past the police cars, twisting wildly to avoid the bashed-in cars involved in the accident. Straight down the middle of the highway on the other side of the bridge he galloped, while Lainey did her best to guide him to the side of the road.

Behind her, she heard the scream of a police car's siren. She couldn't believe it! Was there a policeman in Arizona who didn't understand horses well enough to know it was dangerous to chase them with a siren blaring?

Whiskey lunged forward, straining with all his might to get away from the screaming thing chasing him. Suddenly, he veered off the road into somebody's front yard. He leaped another fence, a high one this time.

Lainey didn't make the leap with him. She lost her balance, fell, and landed on her back with a whomp.

For a while she blacked out. When she came to, a young policeman was standing there with his ticket book open. He looked dismayed. "You all right?" he asked.

"Yes," she said. "Where's Whiskey?"

"The horse? He's over there." The policeman pointed. Whiskey was standing by the swimming pool looking as nonchalant as an invited guest waiting for the party to begin. "I'm giving you a ticket for jumping that barricade," the policeman said.

Lainey stared at his round, beardless face. "You nearly killed me," she said. "You scared my horse half crazy. I didn't jump that thing on purpose. I don't even know how to jump. Whiskey spooked. He didn't expect anything to be on the bridge, and when he saw that barricade, he just took off. I could've stopped him soon enough if you hadn't chased us."

The young policeman looked uncertain. "Well," he said, "all right. I'll let you off this time, but you better not ignore a police barricade again. They're there for a purpose, you know."

She was tempted to reply that he'd better not chase horses with siren blaring again either, but she held her tongue. Her head hurt. She touched the back of it carefully. Nothing wet there that might be blood, fortunately.

Seeing her gesture, the policeman asked anxiously,

"You want to go to the emergency room? Maybe you'd better."

"No, I'm fine." She got to her feet to prove it. "I have to get to a parade. What time is it, please?"

It was seven-thirty. She still could make it. "My father'll be there," she said as the policeman hesitated about letting her go. "He'll take care of me if I need anything."

Sheepishly, he said, "It's my first day on the job."

She unlatched the gate to the pool and collected Whiskey. He was calm now, as he usually was immediately after he'd acted up, Lainey realized. She mounted him, said good-bye to the policeman, and rode off. Actually, she told herself, she'd been lucky no one had come storming out of the house to complain about a horse tearing up their yard.

"You just made it," Amber said when Lainey brought Whiskey to a stop beside her in front of the small stone courthouse.

Lainey's head was throbbing. Her shoulder and hip ached, and she felt nauseous, whether from nerves or the fall she didn't know. "How long is the parade?" she asked, wanting to know how long she had to endure.

"Not more than an hour. Why?"

"I had an accident. Whiskey jumped a fence, and I fell off. Do I look okay?"

"He threw you!" Amber used her bandanna to whisk dirt off Lainey. "There, you don't look too bad. What happened? How did he throw you?"

"It wasn't his fault," Lainey said, and briefly explained about the barricade and the police car.

The square in front of the courthouse steps was a carnival of horses walking around or standing and facing in every direction. Anyone who wanted to ride in the parade was welcome. Little girls had come on ponies, old men in military uniform, ladies in fancy fringed western shirts and boots, kids with a banner from a 4-H club.

The nearest float carried an environmental display of Arizona flora and fauna. Kids on foot in red and white baseball uniforms were getting ordered about by a loud-voiced man. Several people held up homemade banners. A man was shrilly hawking his helium balloons. To add to the excitement, a brass band began tuning up. At the first resonating sounds, horses started side-stepping, backing up, and in one case, rearing. Whiskey stood still, with his ears stretched forward as if he were intrigued.

"Let's go," someone yelled, and a man on a white horse with a flag set off toward the park. A car full of dignitaries followed, and the brass marching band fell in behind the car. The bandsmen wore high red fezzes with tassels. They set off with a drumroll and a blast of horns. Their music was as loud as any Lainey had ever heard.

"This is it," Amber yelled over the tubas. "Let's go."

Whiskey didn't need much encouragement. He responded immediately to Lainey's touch and surged forward eagerly. She let him move up to the front line of riders, just behind the marching band. It took her a minute to figure out that the reason Whiskey's gait felt different was that he was prancing. He was picking his legs up high and holding his head erect, moving like a dancer in time to the music.

She couldn't help but grin despite the pain in her head. Whiskey liked music. What a horse he was! She laughed in delight.

Amber drew up beside her. "Wow," she said. "You didn't tell me he could do that."

"I didn't know," Lainey said.

Whiskey pranced the entire route of the parade. At one point bulbs flashed in Lainey's eyes as a photographer snapped pictures. He stepped up alongside her leg to ask Lainey for her name.

"Is it okay if we print a picture of you and your horse in the paper, Elaine Cobb?"

"Sure," Lainey said, but she was careful to explain that Whiskey belonged to Mr. Dodge.

"Look at that horse, Mommy. Look at that horse dance!" a child squealed in wonder along the route to the park. She was pointing to Whiskey. Lainey sat up straighter, so proud it almost took her headache away.

When they got to the park, she saw that her cheering section had come in full force. There was her father. He stood tall and broad with Ryan and his father and Mr. Dodge, in front of their parked cars. Ryan's smile stretched off his cheeks. He gave her a thumbs-up sign.

Her father's face had a matching grin as he watched her. When had he last grinned that joyously? It had been weeks, months maybe.

Next thing Lainey knew, the parade was abruptly over. Someone on a loudspeaker advised the crowd where refreshments were to be found and said the horse auction was about to begin. Lainey dismounted, introduced Amber to Ryan, and met Ryan's father, who thanked her for single-handedly getting Ryan interested in horses. She denied that but accepted her male supporters' compliments on Whiskey's performance with pleasure. "Where's Mom?" she asked her father.

"Potential customer showed up, so she stayed."

Amber tugged at Lainey's sleeve. "I've got to go," she said. "Dad's meeting me with the horse trailer by the gate, Lainey. Let me know how the auction comes out."

"Okay," Lainey said. She turned to find a stranger leading Whiskey away to the far side of the parking lot, where the horses to be auctioned off were being shown. Instantly, Lainey stopped hearing what was being said to her. She had an urge to stop the man and snatch her horse back. But Whiskey wasn't her horse. She could only stand there helplessly and let him go.

"Let's go watch the auction," Ryan said to his father. The five of them—Lainey and Dad, Mr. Dodge, Ryan and his father—moved into the group of people around the auctioneer, who was standing on a wooden box and holding a microphone. The man had long silver hair and, on his plaid shirt, he wore the fanciest silver and turquoise bolo tie that Lainey had ever seen.

The auctioneer's voice boomed until he adjusted the mike. In rapid order, he put three horses up for bids and sold them to buyers who had apparently examined them already. Lainey's heartbeat picked up until it was going at a gallop when the auctioneer said, "And now, folks, here we go with the star of today's parade— Whiskey. Owner's Roy Dodge, and this handsome, high-stepping young gelding has been part of his riding stock for a year now. What am I bid on Whiskey? Six hundred? Do I hear seven?"

To Lainey's surprise, Ryan's father put in a bid at eight hundred dollars. "Why did he do that?" Lainey asked Ryan.

"Tell you later," he said and went back to listening.

It didn't matter. The bidding moved fast as a skeet shoot. Through it Ryan's father stayed silent. The faint hope his bid had roused in Lainey faded. Someone offered a thousand dollars, eleven hundred, twelve. The final bid came from a skinny blond man in a white cowboy hat and tan Levis.

"Sold," the auctioneer said. Lainey gave one last despairing glance at Ryan's father, but he was asking Ryan if he wanted to get a soda, as if he didn't really care that Whiskey had been sold to a stranger.

Lainey walked up to the young man in the white cowboy hat—Whiskey's new owner.

"Birthday present for my wife," he told her when

Lainey asked him why he'd bought the horse. His mild blue eyes were friendly as he said, "You're the kid that rode him in the parade."

"Yes."

"You did a good job. He's a good horse, huh?"

"Does your wife know much about horses?" Lainey asked.

"Oh, she's ridden all her life. Used to have a show horse when she was a kid."

Mr. Dodge had hobbled over on his cane and was standing at the young man's elbow, waiting to talk to him. "Whiskey acts up sometimes," Lainey warned, ignoring Mr. Dodge. "I mean, he's not bad. He doesn't bite or kick. But he's a character. He'll do things you don't expect."

"Yeah, I can see he's got some fire to him. That's why I picked him for my wife. She likes spirit in an animal." The young man's eyes were sympathetic as he said, "You're kind of stuck on him yourself, huh?"

Lainey nodded and swallowed hard. "Will he have a place to get out of the sun?"

"Sure, his own barn and corral. Don't you worry. He's going to a good home."

She drew a deep breath and took a step back, leaving Mr. Dodge alone to talk business with the young man. This was it, then, Lainey told herself, the best she could expect. She should be glad for Whiskey. It was selfish of her to feel so rotten. Be glad, she ordered herself.

"Lainey, are you feeling all right?" her father asked her.

"My head hurts," she admitted. Now that it didn't matter anymore, she even told him how the policeman had chased her and how she'd fallen again.

"We're taking you to a doctor," Dad announced when she'd finished her story. "See you later," he told the others, who had been listening in. Before Lainey could protest, he hustled her into his truck.

She hadn't even said good-bye to Whiskey, she thought. But maybe that was just as well. She'd already shed too many tears.

"Looks like you're going to get quite a chunk of cash from that horse," Dad said as he maneuvered them through the city streets to the hospital.

"I don't care about that anymore, Daddy."

"I know, honey. I know. Listen, I was so proud of you, the way you handled that animal. I can't remember when I was so proud of anybody."

"Good for a girl, huh, Dad?" she asked slyly.

He glanced at her. "Now, why are you twisting what I'm saying? Did I ever think less of you because you're female?"

"Yes," she said. "You did. You did."

"Not so."

"Then how come you never thought to ask me if *I* wanted to be your business partner, like you asked Lon and Pete?"

"Why—because."

"Because what, Dad?" she pressed him.

He frowned and gunned the engine at a red light. "Never mind," he said, and he looked at her hard. "Just you grow up. And if I've got any business then to offer you a partnership in—and if you still want it—it's yours. Deal?"

"Deal," she said.

She turned toward the window to hide the sudden wash of tears. Crybaby, she taunted herself. You got what you wanted, didn't you—not just Dad's love, but his respect. So what are you crying about? Stop it now. But the tears kept brimming over, and she hurt. Despite all she'd gained, she hurt for what she had lost. Her horse, Whiskey, belonged to somebody else.

14

*S*unday morning Lainey managed to open her eyes and grab the receiver on the first ring. "Did you see your picture in the morning paper?"

"I just rolled out of bed, Amber."

"Well, check the front page. You're on it. The photographer caught Whiskey in midprance with his foreleg up, and you've got a winner's smile. Boy, you're lucky, Lainey! You should thank me for making you go to that parade."

"Thanks," Lainey said. "You were right. It was a good idea."

There was silence on the line. Then Amber said, "You don't sound too thrilled. How come? Didn't Whiskey get sold?"

"Yes. A man bought him for his wife. He said she knows horses."

"You get a good price?" Amber asked.

"More than Mr. Dodge expected."

"Then what's the *matter* with you?" Amber sounded annoyed.

"Nothing. Not a thing." Lainey was even more annoyed that Amber, the horse lover, couldn't figure out what was wrong without being told.

"Oh, I get it. You had a fight with your boooyfriend." Amber drew out the last word in a mocking way.

"Amber," Lainey said, "Ryan isn't my boyfriend. Really."

"Well, he likes you a lot. You can't say he doesn't. I've seen the way he looks at you. He *likes* you, Lainey." The accusation in Amber's voice made everything clear to Lainey.

"Amber, you have Belle," she said. "How can you be jealous of me because you think some boy likes me when you have your own horse and I've lost Whiskey?"

"Oh!" Amber said. "Oh, yeah." There were two beats of silence, and then Amber added, "I'm sorry."

Lainey nodded at the phone, relieved that they finally understood each other again. "Okay," she said. "So I'll see you later?"

"Yeah," Amber said and hung up.

Lainey got dressed and dragged herself to the kitchen, feeling as old as Mr. Dodge. Dad was busily cutting up the newspaper. He greeted her with an outsize smile. "Look at this, Lainey. I'm going to hang a copy in my truck. Impress everybody with my famous daughter."

The photo of Whiskey was wonderful, Lainey

thought, but she was all grin and hat. "I look like a little kid," she said.

Dad hugged her and teased, "Yeah, but you got to admit it's a good picture of the hat."

Mom sauntered into the room and over to the coffee-pot in her Sunday attire—zoris, queen-size shorts, and an extra large man's T-shirt. She, too, had a big smile for Lainey. "Congratulations," she said. "I only wish I'd known you were going to be the star of that parade. I would've put those customers off till later and gone to watch you, especially since they weren't serious lookers."

"It wasn't that big a deal, Mom," Lainey said. "Just a kind of thrown-together parade that anybody could enter."

"But your father says you were really something to see," Mom said.

"Not me," Lainey said, "Whiskey. He was the big surprise. I didn't even know he could prance. He stayed in step with the marching band the whole way."

Before she'd finished eating the celebration pancakes Mom insisted on making her, Ryan called. "I didn't think you knew my phone number," Lainey said.

"I didn't. I called Mr. Dodge. And before we forget, you better write down my number." He dictated his telephone number and address and she dutifully wrote them down.

"My father thinks you've got the right stuff," Ryan said then. "In fact, my status went up a notch just for being your humble student."

"Ryan, you teach me things, too."

"Like what?"

"Umm, I don't know. Don't bug me this early in the morning when I can't think straight." The praise pouring in from every direction was making her cranky for some reason.

"Sorry. So anyway, congratulations. You were splendid, as the English would say."

"No," she said. "Whiskey was."

"How come you sound so low?" Before it could burst out of her, he answered himself. "Yeah . . . oh . . . sure." Ryan packed a heavy weight of sympathy into each separate word. "It's too bad Dad's bid was low."

"Why *did* he bid on Whiskey?" she asked.

"Remember I told you he had a surprise for me? The surprise was he wants to buy me a horse. He figures now that I've begun to like riding, it'd be a bribe for me to spend my vacations out here with him. In fact, he came right out and said so."

"He must really love you, Ryan."

"Think so? I guess he must want me around for some reason, huh?"

"Yeah, some reason," she said. "Unless he just wants to save you from an overdose of literature."

"That's the girl!" Ryan said. "You're feeling better already. I can tell."

She wasn't, but she chatted with him for a few more minutes before she ended the conversation. Afterward, she considered what would have happened if Ryan had become Whiskey's owner. The good thing about it for her would have been that she might have seen Whiskey again. The bad thing would have been for Whiskey to get only a part-time master. Who would have taken care of him when Ryan wasn't around? Unless Ryan's father meant to do that. But it didn't matter now, anyway. The skinny blond man had been the higher bidder, much higher. And his wife knew horses. Whiskey would be better off with a full-time owner like her.

The next caller was Mr. Dodge. "Did you see yourself on the front page of the paper?" he asked. "I'd send you my copy, but I'd sort of like to keep it for myself."

"That's all right, Mr. Dodge. We got a copy." And Dad had just left to buy more, saying he wanted to send them to Lainey's brothers.

"Well, fine," Mr. Dodge said. "Now when are you coming by to collect your money? Young feller gave me a check. Him and his wife come this morning with a horse van to take Whiskey away. Thought we might have trouble getting Whiskey into that van, but he climbed right up the ramp like he'd done it before. Maybe he had. Don't know how his life was before I bought him."

"So Whiskey's gone?" Lainey's heart lurched. "Do they live near here?"

"The young couple? No. Out by the Desert Museum someplace."

"Oh," Lainey said. The Desert Museum was way on the other side of town. "Did she seem nice?"

"Eh? Well, she liked the look of your horse. Rode him around and said he was a nice stepper."

"And did Whiskey seem to like her?"

"I couldn't say, Lainey. He behaved himself though. . . . You know, I don't know how you managed to train that animal, spoiling him the way you did, but it sure worked. Can't say it didn't."

"I'll be by, Mr. Dodge," Lainey said. "I don't know just when."

Days passed. Lainey kept delaying going to pick up her money from Mr. Dodge. She didn't want to see the emptied corral without Whiskey in it.

"You know," Dad said, "we could fix the fence around the backyard in the new place and rebuild that old shed so you could stable a horse in it. How much is Dodge giving you? Enough to buy a horse?"

"Maybe. I don't know exactly, Daddy." How could she think about another horse when she was still mourning the loss of the one she'd had?

Thursday, Mr. Dodge called her. "You better get over here, Lainey. We got a problem."

She was helping Mom pack dishes for their move, which was to take place on Saturday, but she left the packing and hiked down the road. It was eleven o'clock in the morning, and the temperature was already up to 105. Her perspiration dried before it could dampen her shirt. She hustled along, feeling nauseous and light-headed in turn. So close to high noon, she should have brought water with her on even this short a walk. But for once she'd forgotten.

The instant she spotted Whiskey standing in the shade of the open shed roof with four or five of the oldest horses, her spirits rose. She didn't stop to wonder why he was there—she was too glad to see him. The old two-note whistle brought him ambling to the corral fence. He was as calm as if they had never been parted.

"If I'd known you were here, I'd have brought you some bread," Lainey told him. "I missed you, Whiskey. I missed you so much." She kissed his forehead.

"Lainey, come in here. I got to talk to you," Mr. Dodge called from his office.

She left Whiskey reluctantly and went to the office. "Why's he back, Mr. Dodge?"

He switched off the TV and offered her the narrow chair Dad had sat in. "Seems Whiskey's acting up. The wife called. Said all the neighbors is mad at them because he keeps leaping the paddock fence and getting into their yards and eating their plantings. Also, he's gone back to his old tricks of turning around when she wants to take him on a trail ride. She says he shies when she whips him." Mr. Dodge rubbed the back of his neck. "I give the feller his money back, Lainey."

"Good. Whiskey shouldn't be whipped. No wonder he won't go for her." Lainey was indignant. "I thought her husband said she knew horses. Some horsewoman she must be!"

"Yeah, but now we got a horse and no money. I was

thinking you could call your friend Ryan, maybe. See if his dad still wants to buy Whiskey. I'd take that bid now and be glad to get it. Of course, you wouldn't be making much on his offer."

"Do you have Ryan's telephone number here?" she asked. High on a wave of newfound energy, she couldn't wait to ask Ryan.

The phone rang, and rang again, and rang a third time. She fidgeted anxiously. Wasn't he there? If he spent all his time reading the way he claimed, he should be there.

Finally, Ryan answered. He sounded glad to hear her voice. "Lainey, hi. How're you doing?"

"Fine, but there's a problem with Whiskey." Without trying to hide anything, she explained it. "Do you think your father would buy him anyway? I mean, would you want him even with his tricks?"

"I'll talk to Dad tonight," Ryan said. "He might still be willing. He's been looking into other horses for me."

"But Ryan, what if Whiskey runs away on you, too? And what if you can't make him go more than a quarter of a mile, either?"

"Don't worry. I know the way to his heart. I'll stuff him with apples and carrots and bread, and curry him just like you did."

"And talk to him. He likes to listen."

"Sure. I'll read him Shakespeare. Or would he prefer someone more modern? Dr. Seuss, maybe?"

"Oh, Ryan! But even if your father says okay, what happens to Whiskey when you go back to New York?"

"Don't worry. We'll think of something. Let me talk to Dad and see what he says."

Lainey couldn't help worrying. She worried her way back home to continue helping her mother with the packing. While Lainey's hands put things in cartons, her head was busy working out Whiskey's future. One idea she had was to pay for an ad in the paper that would mention his parade fame and offer him for sale to an owner—subject to Whiskey's personal approval. People who really loved horses might consider that a challenge. Unless they thought it was weird. And who would pay money for a horse that obeyed only when he felt like it?

Ryan's phone call caught her as she was about to leave the house to take Whiskey for a sunset ride.

"Okay," Ryan said after they'd exchanged greetings, "here's the deal. Dad will make good on his original offer to Dodge if you can take care of Whiskey for us when I'm not in town."

"Are you serious, Ryan?"

"You like it, huh?"

"I can't believe it. That'd be so great! But we're moving, and how would I get to your place? It's too far to walk."

"Listen, Dad's going to bring me over to Dodge's on his way to the hospital tomorrow morning, and we'll work out the details. There's got to be a way to do this. Maybe you can keep him at the ranch."

"I won't be close enough to walk there anymore. But you know what? There's room behind the house we're renting. There's even an old shed and a fence. It needs repair, but I could use my own money for materials and Dad would do the work. Oh, Ryan! . . . But what do you get out of this?"

"What do you mean? Don't you think I can train Whiskey to like me? I'm a nice guy. We'll get along. You just tell him I'm a friend of yours."

"You are my friend," she said.

Amber was right, Lainey realized after the phone call. Ryan did like her a lot. And he was a boy and smart and cute. And even if he came from New York and read novels for fun, they had something in common, something important—Whiskey, her horse, their horse. She gave a joyous shout and ran to tell her mother, who was sorting linens, and then her father, who was packing tools from the utility closet. Finally, she flew down the road to the ranch.

"Whiskey," she called when she saw him waiting for her at the corral fence. "Whiskey, I've got the best news!"